Dawn felt fresh waves of horror engulf her. Was Rob right? Had she had an epileptic seizure in front of half the school?

"Probably not," Dr. Weinstein said.

"Then what?"

The doctor glanced at Dawn lying rigid on the bed. "Perhaps it would be best to talk in the hall."

"No," Dawn's mother said. "Dawn's been through too much for us all to retreat and leave her alone just now. We don't keep secrets from her. She's entitled to hear what you say."

Dawn's heart swelled with gratitude toward her mother for remembering her promise to never keep the truth from her—no matter how bad or scary it might be.

"Very well," Dr. Weinstein said. "I'm positive that your daughter has had a stroke."

To Live Again

Lurlene McDaniel

To Live Again

Bought by: Maura Barry
Given to: Maura Barry

November 15, 2001

BANTAM BOOKS
NEW YORK • TORONTO • LONDON • SYDNEY • AUCKLAND

RL: 5.3, AGES 12 AND UP

TO LIVE AGAIN

A Bantam Book / April 2001

Text copyright © 2001 by Lurlene McDaniel
Cover art copyright © 2001 by Ericka O'Rourke

ISBN: 0-553-57151-6

Visit us on the Web! www.randomhouse.com/teens
Educators and librarians, for a variety of teaching tools, visit us at
www.randomhouse.com/teachers

Published simultaneously in the United States and Canada

Bantam Books is an imprint of Random House Children's Books, a division of
Random House, Inc. BANTAM BOOKS and the rooster colophon are
registered trademarks of Random House, Inc. Bantam Books, 1540 Broadway,
New York, New York 10036.

PRINTED IN THE UNITED STATES OF AMERICA

OPM   10 9 8 7 6 5 4 3 2

This book is dedicated to all my readers
who have asked repeatedly for
"one more book about Dawn Rochelle."
Thank you for caring.
You are the best!

Chapter One

❧ ❧

"Tell me, Squirt, is being a senior at Hardy as good as you thought it would be?"

Dawn Rochelle looked up from her homework, which was spread across the kitchen table, and made a face at her brother, Rob. If anyone else had called her Squirt, she'd have decked them, but it was Rob's favorite nickname for his kid sister, so Dawn tolerated it. The connection between them was special—Rob's bone marrow had saved her life.

"Being a senior is no different from being a junior," she answered. "Except there's more homework."

"A snap for a brain like you."

"That's me, all right, the Brain." Dawn leaned back in her chair. "And a pretty dulled brain right now. Sit down. Talk to me."

Rob pulled out a chair. "Can't stay but a minute. Just popped in on my way home. Mom said you're applying to Ohio State. True?"

"It has a great medical school. I'd like to study medicine."

"I would have thought you'd have had enough of things medical and would want to go into anything *except* medicine."

Dawn knew exactly what Rob meant. Leukemia when she was thirteen, a bone marrow transplant when she was fourteen, and periodic checkups to ensure that her new bone marrow was still cancer-free had been the focus of her life for years. But now that she was approaching the three-year remission mark, she almost thought of herself as normal. Almost. "I'm leaving my medical miseries behind," she replied. "Time for payback. I want to help others the way I've been helped."

"I'm proud of you, Squirt."

She tipped her chin and studied him through half-closed eyes. "Wait a sec. You want something, don't you?"

"Me?" He feigned innocence. "Can't I pay my favorite sister a compliment?"

"Your *only* sister," she corrected. "Come on . . . what do you want me to do?"

"Well, since you ask, I was wondering if you'd

baby-sit Keegan Friday night so I can take Katie out to dinner and a movie."

The mention of her six-month-old nephew made Dawn feel gooey inside. No one was cuter than Keegan, with his big blue eyes and curly red hair. "He looks enough like you to be yours!" Dawn's mother had exclaimed the night he was born, when Dawn and her parents had stood gazing at him through the nursery's plate glass window. Dawn's heart had constricted with her mother's words. Dawn's chemotherapy had more than likely left her sterile—it was doubtful she'd ever be able to have children of her own.

"I might be available," Dawn told Rob now.

"I wouldn't want to keep you from a hot date or anything."

"Not a problem," Dawn said. "There's an away football game, but I'm not going."

"Then you're hired," Rob said with a grin.

"Can Rhonda tag along?" Dawn's best friend had had a crush on Rob for ages, until he had married Katie the summer between the girls' sophomore and junior years.

"It breaks my heart," Rhonda had said with a resigned sigh. "But I know when it's over for me. I was just born too late."

Dawn had patted Rhonda on the head. "You'll

get over it." And of course Rhonda had. She lusted after every cute guy at Hardy High but had yet to land a steady boyfriend.

"Sure. Just no wild parties," Rob said with a wink.

"I'll cancel the band."

Rob stood, ruffled her hair, and kissed her forehead. "Thanks, Squirt."

Dawn almost told him to cool it with the nickname, but he was gone from the kitchen before she could speak up. She looked down at the heap of books on the table, sighed, and returned to her homework.

"The baby's been fed and bathed, honey. You just have to give him a bottle before bedtime. I left our cell phone number posted on the fridge. Don't hesitate to call if you have *any* problems." Katie put on earrings as she talked to Dawn over her shoulder.

"I will." Dawn juggled her gurgling nephew while following Katie out of the bedroom as she gave last-minute instructions.

From the living room, Rob called out, "She can handle it, Katie. Come on—our reservations are for six and we're not going to make it."

"Of course we'll make it." Katie kissed Rob's cheek and offered a radiant smile. "I'm not about to miss our first real date in weeks." She turned to Dawn. "Any questions?"

"Hmm . . . how about what's the origin of the universe? Or does time ever travel backward?"

"Cute," Rob said.

"Don't worry. Go have fun. Keegan and I are going to have a great time together." Keegan grinned, showing off his only tooth. "Now go," Dawn said to Rob and Katie.

"Did I tell you where his nighttime diapers are?"

"Three times," Rob said, taking his wife's elbow and leading her to the car. He seated her in the car and shut the door firmly.

Dawn stood on the porch and waggled the baby's arm as the car backed out of the driveway. "Wave bye-bye."

Inside the house again, she cooed at Keegan, "For a nurse, your mommy is such a worrywart." Katie had been Dawn's nurse in the hospital, which was where she and Rob had met. Dawn was crazy about her sister-in-law and thought Rob's marriage to Katie had been one smart move. She sat on the sofa and was playing patty-cake with Keegan when the doorbell rang.

"It's me to the rescue," Rhonda said dramatically, sweeping into the room. "I've got two videos."

"I don't need rescuing. I need company," Dawn told her.

"Believe me, girl, when you take baby-sitting over the opportunity to watch Jake play tonight, you need rescuing."

"I thought we weren't going to talk about that." Dawn returned to the sofa with Keegan.

"*You* weren't going to talk about it. I made no such promise."

Dawn groaned. "Look, Rhonda, Jake and I are just friends. I'm not going to chase after him like some ditsy girl."

In truth, Dawn didn't want to talk about her real reason for not going to the game. She had rounded a corner at school midweek and had seen Jake and Tasha Lewis having a close encounter under the stairwell. Tasha had been giving him one of her famous seductive looks, and Jake had appeared to be lapping it up. Dawn's blood had run hot and cold as she watched them together. Dawn had adored Jake Macka since fifth grade, and during the past couple of years they'd hung around together, but now she believed that he was growing tired of her and that friends were really all they would ever be. She had avoided him all week—better than getting dumped, she'd figured.

"Okay," Rhonda said. "Let's forget about you

6

and Jake. Let's talk about me and Ed Silverman, Jake's good buddy. I have a thing for him."

"You have a thing for all Jake's football buddies. And in the spring, you'll have a thing for his soccer buddies."

"One of them has got to notice me eventually." Rhonda grinned. "I'm so adorable."

Dawn giggled. "Yes, you are. But so is Keegan."

"Are you comparing me to a baby?"

Dawn started to say something, but all of a sudden she felt woozy. The room began to spin, and her vision blurred.

"You all right?" Rhonda's question sounded as if it were coming through a tunnel.

"Take the baby," Dawn mumbled. "I—I have a terrible headache. And my hand's all numb."

Chapter
Two

❧ ❧

Dawn felt as if a knife were stabbing into the right side of her skull. Her blurred vision cleared, but suddenly she was seeing double—two of everything in any direction she looked.

"Lie down!" Rhonda commanded, snatching Keegan away from Dawn. The baby began to cry.

Dawn lay on the sofa and closed her eyes, willing the room to stop spinning. Finally, the pain subsided, and she opened her eyes. The room was in perfect focus. Rhonda looked white as a sheet.

"I—I'm all right," Dawn said, attempting to sit up.

Rhonda pushed her down. "Make sure. Don't get up too fast."

"The baby's crying. We scared him."

"Keegan's fine." Rhonda stroked the baby's

cheeks and hunted for his pacifier. "What happened to you?"

"I don't know. All of a sudden, I got this headache and the room started going round. But it's over. I'll take the baby."

"No way. You might drop him."

Dawn flexed her left hand, which felt tingly. "Maybe you're right. His bottle's in the fridge. Can you warm it and give it to him?"

"Only if you promise to lie still."

"I'm okay now, Rhonda."

"Stay put," Rhonda insisted. She took the baby with her to the kitchen, where Dawn heard her fumbling around for the bottle.

Dawn tried to make sense of what had happened and couldn't. She'd never experienced such weird symptoms before, not even when she'd first come down with leukemia. Her heart thudded. *What if . . . No*, she told herself. No use becoming paranoid. According to her tests, leukemia was behind her, a thing of the past. Whatever had happened to her tonight was not related to cancer.

By the time Rhonda returned, Dawn was sitting up. Her tongue felt thick and her left hand heavy, but otherwise, she was all right. "Maybe I'm just tired," she offered.

9

"Yeah, maybe." Rhonda sat in a rocker and fed Keegan, who soon nodded off. "I'll take him upstairs," she said.

Dawn watched her go, wishing she was the one carrying her nephew and putting him to bed. She couldn't explain what had happened to her, and at the moment she felt perfectly fine. Still, the whole episode had been strange. She picked up the television remote and started flipping through the channels.

"How was the rest of your weekend?" The words were out of Rhonda's mouth before she plopped her tray next to Dawn's in the cafeteria on Monday.

"Boring. How was yours?"

"My dad dragged us off for a weekend getaway." Rhonda poked suspiciously at her food. "Talk about boring. What I want to know is, did you have any more spells?"

" 'Spells'? You make it sound like something from a Jane Austen book. Or from a voodoo curse."

"Hello, Dawn. People don't just get sudden headaches and fall over. I'm worried, that's all." Rhonda sniffed indignantly.

Dawn knew she was giving her friend a hard time, but she didn't want to dwell on the episode. "It happened. It's over. Let's forget about it."

"You did tell your mother, didn't you?"

"Rhonda. It didn't happen again, so I saw no reason to report to Mom. You know how hyper she gets." Wanting to divert Rhonda's attention from the topic, Dawn leaned over and whispered, "Look left. Ed just came into the cafeteria."

Her ploy worked. Rhonda whipped around. "Be still my heart," she sighed. "He's *so* adorable."

Ed stood talking to Jake and Tasha. The pretty blond senior was batting her eyes at both of the guys. Dawn made a show of eating her lunch, which had suddenly lost its appeal.

"Would you just look at that girl?" Rhonda muttered. "Rubbing up against them like a cat at a scratching post. Doesn't she know Jake is taken?"

Dawn felt her face grow warm. "He's a free agent."

"He shouldn't be."

"Can we not talk about this now?"

"You don't want to talk about anything today."

"Listen, Rhonda, we can talk later, someplace less public."

Rhonda grabbed Dawn's arm. "Red alert. Jake's heading our way."

Dawn braced herself.

"Hey, stranger," Jake said, sliding into the chair directly across the table from Dawn.

11

"Hi yourself."

"Missed you at the game Friday night."

"I had to baby-sit. But I read that your extra point won the game."

Rhonda stood abruptly. "I think I hear art class calling me."

Dawn wished Rhonda would hang around. "Call you after school, okay?"

"Is it something I said?" Jake asked, watching Rhonda scurry away.

"No. She's irked at me." Alone with Jake looking across the table at her, Dawn felt self-conscious. The gaze of his big brown eyes could always turn her into quivering jelly, and this moment was no exception.

He asked, "What gives? You've been avoiding me for days."

"Not true. I've been busy."

"Too busy to even talk to me when I call? I did last night, and your mother said you couldn't come to the phone."

Dawn had known it was Jake because Caller ID was on all the home phones, but she had shouted "I'm washing my hair" when her mother had told her she had a call. The image of Jake and Tasha beneath the stairwell had burned itself into her brain, and she couldn't get it out. Dawn knew she wasn't as pretty as Tasha, and although Jake had

12

always been kind to Dawn, he didn't treat her as though she was the great love of his life.

Jake reached over and touched the ends of her auburn hair. "Squeaky clean."

Her knees went weak. Of course, Jake would remember when chemo had made all her long hair fall out. She still had the get-well card he'd sent her when she'd been hospitalized. During the year of her bone marrow transplant, his family had moved from Columbus, and they had returned only when Jake and Dawn had both been sophomores. They'd hung around together off and on during the previous couple of years, but it was obvious to Dawn that she liked him a whole lot more than he liked her.

"Why don't you let me drive you home from school today?" he asked.

Her pulse quickened, then slowed. He'd driven her home many times, but nothing had ever come of it. "Sure. I have gym class last period, so—"

"I know." He grinned in his lopsided way. "I'll wait for you to do whatever it takes you girls so long to do after gym class."

She blushed and wondered how fast she could perform a complete makeover after forty-five minutes of playing lacrosse, the fall sport Mrs. Hadley was forcing on the senior girls. "We could meet at my locker," Dawn said, suddenly remembering that Tasha also had gym class last period. She didn't want Tasha and Jake running into each other while she was stuck in the bathroom making repairs. Of course, Tasha never did anything more constructive than put on lipstick.

"I know where that is too," he said. "Come on, the bell's about to ring." He stood.

Dawn started to stand, but her left leg refused to obey. "Uh—go on. I'll catch up."

"You okay?"

A film of perspiration broke out on her forehead. "Fine." She boosted herself and lifted her tray with her right hand. Her left hand suddenly felt like a lead weight. The room began to sway. She lurched, and the tray went spinning out of control. It hit the floor with a crash that made every person in the room turn her way.

"What's wrong?" Jake took her elbow.

"I—I don't know. I can't lift my arm." Her muscles refused to operate, and she felt her legs turn rubbery.

Jake bolstered her. "Here, lean on me."

Dawn started a slow slide toward the floor.

He caught her and lifted her as if she were a rag doll. She heard him shout, "Quick! Somebody call 911!"

14

Chapter
Three
✎

In the ambulance, Dawn lay terrified as the siren screeched. Medics hovered over her, poking an IV in her arm, taking her pulse and blood pressure. Her sweater and T-shirt were removed and electrodes were taped to her chest. Covered loosely by a blanket, she felt exposed and humiliated. She couldn't lift her left hand, and the numbness kept spreading up her arm. Tears made a path down her cheeks.

"Your parents have been called," one paramedic said, as if she'd asked him a question. Had she? She tried to speak, but her tongue felt thick, unresponsive.

At the hospital, the ambulance doors were thrown open and she was rolled inside the emergency room. There she was lifted onto another stretcher, and a new team of doctors and nurses peered down at her. "Can you squeeze my hand?" a physician asked.

"Dawn . . . it *is* Dawn, isn't it? Can you tell me what day of the week this is?"

She tried to focus, but her brain seemed to be in a fog. Numbness crept up her arm and down her side. The world was out of control.

"Your parents are on their way, Dawn," a nurse told her.

A second nurse said, "I know this girl. She's Katie Rochelle's sister-in-law."

More electrodes and wires were placed on Dawn's head and chest. "Get her to radiology," a doctor ordered. "I want head X rays and a CAT scan."

An orderly rolled her gurney down the hall. Overhead, the lights flashed past, and sounds seemed to be coming from far away. In minutes, the orderly stopped and pressed a button, opening double doors. "I'll be back for you," he said.

In the darkened radiology department, a technician told her, "We're going to do a CAT scan, Dawn. Do you know what that is?"

She nodded. At least she could still do that much.

"Good," he said. "Then you know you have to lie very still."

She was transferred to a hard metal table with

a hulking machine at its head. The tec... stepped behind a glass wall, and the machine began to move slowly along her body, enveloping her in a smooth metal tunnel. She concentrated on the whirring the machine made, not on her feeling of panic over the tomblike encasement and her sense of being swallowed alive. Memories of her past treatments for leukemia rose up to haunt her. The spinal taps, the chemo protocols, the nausea and vomiting, the specter of death hanging over her—these were the legacy of cancer. And now it might be happening all over. She wasn't sure she could go through it again.

The CAT scan ended, and the technician took traditional X rays of her head and upper body. "I'll get these to the ER right away," he said, patting her left shoulder. With a start, Dawn realized she no longer had feeling in her shoulder.

She was returned to the ER, where another doctor introduced himself as a neurologist. He asked her questions, but she was having trouble making her voice work. Her mind kept begging, *What's wrong with me? Please tell me!* But the ability to ask the question evaded her, and the neurologist couldn't read her mind.

The neurologist asked, "Have you had any problems with your vision during the last couple of days?"

…izzy spells?"

…nod.

…y numbness or tingling in your arm?"

She hated having to answer yes to each of his questions.

"But the symptoms cleared up, right?"

She agreed, realizing that whatever was happening to her now had given her warning signals that she had ignored. But at the time, the signs had seemed isolated and inconsequential. She'd had phantom pains many times after going through recovery from her bone marrow transplant. Fear could set them off, so she struggled hard not to give in to fear. Ever since her transplant, she'd spent a lot of mental energy building a wall of positive thinking around her. *I'm cured; I can no longer be touched by cancer*, she would tell herself whenever a pain or a fever would come on her. She still took antirejection drugs that enabled Rob's bone marrow to become her own. She believed she was well, and her checkups had all been good. What was happening to her now made no sense.

"Dawn, I want you to move your left arm."

She tried to do what the doctor asked, but her arm wouldn't respond. Fresh tears pooled in her eyes.

"It's all right, Dawn. Take it easy. We'll try again later."

A commotion in the doorway caused the doctor to look up. "Where's our daughter?" Dawn heard her father ask.

Suddenly Dawn was surrounded by her family, and the sight of their faces made her weak with relief. Her mother leaned over her and kissed her forehead. "We're here, honey," she said. "We're here, and everything will be all right now."

Dawn longed to believe her mother.

"What's going on?" Dawn's father demanded. "What happened to her?"

Before the doctor could say a word, Rob and Katie rushed into the area. The expression on her family's faces reflected the fear Dawn was feeling.

"I'm Dr. Weinstein," the neurologist said to the group. "Apparently your daughter passed out at school."

"Why?" Dawn's father asked.

"That's what we're trying to determine. We've done blood work and a CAT scan. Now I want an EEG." He picked up his notepad. "Has she ever had seizures?"

"No," Dawn's mother said. "But she has had leukemia and a bone marrow transplant."

"You don't think this has anything to do with

cancer, do you?" Rob's voice cut through the noise of the ER.

Dawn understood Rob's concern. He'd always worried that his marrow would be rejected by her body and that it would be his fault if she died.

Dr. Weinstein jotted notes. "Then she's had a lot of chemo?"

"Yes, but that was years ago," Dawn's mother said. "She had a checkup a month ago, before school started. Everything was fine."

"I don't think what's happened today is related to her history of cancer," the doctor said.

"Thank God," her mother said, her shoulders heaving. She smoothed Dawn's hair off her forehead.

"So then, what is it? Epilepsy?" Rob asked.

Until that moment, epilepsy hadn't crossed Dawn's mind. She didn't know much about the condition, but she remembered that in second grade a boy named Herb had had a grand mal seizure in her classroom. He sat behind her, and one day, during a spelling test, she'd heard him making gurgling sounds. She'd turned to look and saw him fall to the floor, legs stiff and body rigid. While other kids had jumped up and even cried, Dawn had simply stared. Herb's eyes were rolled back in his head, and his body made grotesque jerking motions. The teacher had rushed forward, commanding everyone to stand back. She'd knelt, cushioned Herb's head with her sweater, and shoved desks out of the way so that he wouldn't hit them as he thrashed on the floor. When the convulsions had finally stopped and Herb had gone limp, Dawn could see that he had wet himself. The teacher had helped him up and taken him out of the room. He didn't return to class for a week, and when he did, some kids made fun of him.

Dawn felt fresh waves of horror engulf her. Was Rob right? Had she had an epileptic seizure in front of half the school?

"Probably not," Dr. Weinstein said.

"Then what?"

The doctor glanced at Dawn lying rigid on the bed. "Perhaps it would be best to talk in the hall."

"No," Dawn's mother said. "Dawn's been through too much for us all to retreat and leave her alone just now. We don't keep secrets from her. She's entitled to hear what you say."

Dawn's heart swelled with gratitude toward her mother for remembering her promise to never keep the truth from her—no matter how bad or scary it might be.

"Very well," Dr. Weinstein said. "I'm positive that your daughter has had a stroke."

Chapter
Four

❧ *❧*

"A stroke?" Dawn heard her father say. "You can't be serious. She's only seventeen years old. Old people have strokes, not kids in the prime of life!"

"It's rare, but it happens," Dr. Weinstein said.

"But she's never had high blood pressure—" her mother started.

"Or high cholesterol," Katie added.

"Those are two leading causes of strokes, but not the only ones. And there are different types of strokes too—"

Rob interrupted. "How can you be sure it's a stroke?" Dawn could trust her big brother always to challenge any doctor. He'd had a difficult time accepting her diagnosis of cancer years before.

"Her CAT scan is showing irregularities. Plus,

I've spoken with Dawn," Dr. Weinstein answered. "Evidently she's had some warning signs. We call them TIAs—transient ischemic attacks, a disturbance in brain function that results when the blood supply is temporarily cut off."

All heads turned toward Dawn on the gurney. "Is this true?" her mother asked her. "Why didn't you say something?"

Dr. Weinstein put his hand on Dawn's shoulder. "The signs would be easy for her to miss, especially since she's so young and strokes are rare in the young."

"But her health has always been an issue. She knows to come to us about any irregularities."

Dawn wanted to cry out, "Don't be mad at me, Mom," but she still couldn't make her voice work. Tears of frustration slid down her cheek.

"It's okay, honey." Katie wiped the tears away, then turned to the others. "She doesn't need this now."

"Of course, you're right. I'm sorry, baby," Dawn's mother said.

"What are you going to do?" her father asked the doctor.

"Admit her," Dr. Weinstein answered. "She needs further testing and evaluating to see how much damage has been done."

"And then?"

"One step at a time," the doctor said. "One step at a time."

Dawn lay flat on her back in a hospital bed, the side railings pulled up, in a room with another bed that was unoccupied. She felt like a baby in a crib—except that she was no baby. She was a teenage girl with paralysis creeping along the left side of her body. She tried to move her fingers and couldn't. She was too scared to try and raise her leg. If it didn't work, then it meant the whole left side of her body was paralyzed.

Her mother bent over the bed and wiped Dawn's face with a damp washcloth. "It's all right, baby. Everything's going to be all right."

You don't know that! Dawn's thoughts screamed, but her voice stayed mute. When was it going to end? When was it going to be over? Would her other side become paralyzed too? Would she become a vegetable, unable to move? Speak? Stand up and walk? What if her lungs became paralyzed? Would they have to put her on a breathing machine? Would she have to spend the rest of her life hooked to machines?

"You've got a good doctor." Katie peered down at Dawn. "I've been asking around—you know, polling my nurse friends. Dr. Weinstein is one of the top neurologists in the area. He takes care of plenty of stroke victims, and he'll take good care of you, too."

"I know you're scared." Her mother again. "We're all scared, but they'll get to the bottom of this, honey. They're sending for all your records. I told them they'd better send a truck." Her mother's attempt at humor made Katie smile, but all Dawn could think of was how long it might take for the doctor to wade through all the reports, charts, and tests from the time she was first hospitalized at thirteen.

"And they'll be doing more tests," Katie said. "You're scheduled for an MRI at eight tonight."

Just how long had it been since she'd collapsed at school? Dawn wondered. That normal world of school and friends and classes seemed far away, like a picture postcard she'd been sent in the mail. She could see the photo, but she wasn't in it. She should be sitting in her afternoon classes, not lying in the hospital, unable to move. And Jake . . . Her heart lurched. He was to have driven her home today. The memory returned in a flash. She pictured his smile. He'd always been able to melt her heart with that smile. What must he have thought when she'd fallen, her lunch tray clattering against the floor?

Her mind fogged again, and she couldn't

remember much except for the ambulance ride and the ER. It was probably better to not remember.

"We won't leave you alone, Dawn," her mother said. "Your dad's down getting a bite of supper. I'll go eat when he returns. I plan to stay the night with you."

"My next-door neighbor has Keegan," Katie said. "I'll have to go home tonight, but I'll be back tomorrow just as soon as I can make arrangements for someone to watch him all day."

Dawn knew her family was trying to be helpful, trying hard to anticipate questions they thought she might have. She appreciated it; however, she had a million questions, so they could never anticipate them all, and without a voice to speak—

"Hey, Squirt. How're you doing?" Rob leaned over the bed and touched the tip of her nose with his finger. "Did you think I'd gone off and left you?"

She hadn't.

"Well, guess where I've been? They have this medical library in the hospital, and of course computers hooked to the Internet. So your bro has been digging around and collecting info about strokes. I know Dr. Weinstein will want to wait for test results and all, but I figured it couldn't hurt to know a little something about the enemy you're up against. What do you think?"

"I don't know, Rob," Katie began.

"Just general info," Rob said. "Nothing scary."

Dawn grunted, hoping to let them know that she was interested in hearing what Rob had to say.

"I'll take that as a yes," Rob said, and rustled a sheaf of papers. "For starters, a person can have more than one kind of stroke—caused by everything from clogged arteries to arteries with thin walls. Your doc will eventually get around to figuring out what kind you had." He shuffled through more papers. "The good news is that people recover from strokes. It can take a little time and some rehab work, but a lot of people recover completely. And I figure with you being so young and all, well, you've got the best chance of all for a total recovery."

He grinned, as if this news was supposed to put her mind at total ease.

"That's good news, isn't it, dear?" her mother asked.

Rob continued. "You'll get a ton of therapists to help you along. Physical therapists, speech therapists, occupational therapists, and even a recreational therapist can be brought in. As if a kid your age needs to be told how to have fun."

She knew he was trying to make her feel better, but the thought of dealing with so many people overwhelmed her. Why couldn't she just start back with her schoolwork without a therapist's help? This was her senior year. She wanted to graduate. She wanted to go to college. How long was her recovery going to take?

"And you don't have to be stuck in the hospital the whole time either." Rob turned to Katie. "Isn't that right, hon?"

"It's true you can do a lot of the work as an outpatient." Katie didn't sound as certain or as enthusiastic as Rob. "I have several professional friends who work as therapists."

Just then a nurse came into the room and said, "It's time for medications." She slipped a needle into Dawn's IV line, and instantly Dawn felt the drug numbing her mind and body. The last thing she heard clearly was the nurse saying to her family, "Listen, what Dawn needs now is rest and quiet. Dr. Weinstein doesn't want her agitated in any way, and frankly, it would be in her best interests if you limited your visits to ten minutes at a time, no more than two people at a time."

Dawn thought she heard Rob start to protest, but Katie shushed him. Then blessed sleep overtook Dawn, and she slipped farther down the rabbit hole, like Alice in search of the white rabbit racing to keep a date on a pocket watch with no face.

28

Chapter
Five

Dawn awoke in the middle of the night, totally disoriented. Although the room was dark, she could see her mother's shape in the sleeping chair beside her bed. Instantly her thoughts returned to the time she'd been in the hospital awaiting her bone marrow transplant. She'd been in isolation, her body radiated and depleted of its ability to ward off germs, even something as simple as a common cold. At the time, she'd been fighting for her life. But now . . . now she didn't know what she was supposed to be fighting for. And worse, she wasn't sure how much fight she had left in her. Weren't the bad times supposed to be behind her?

Stroke. The word tumbled through her mind. It had many meanings, and she tried hard to remember them. A soft, tender touch. The movement of an oar through water toward a goal. A massive brain seizure that leaves a person's body paralyzed, her mind numb. Renewed fear drained away what little energy Dawn had.

A strip of light fell across the foot of Dawn's bed, and a nurse materialized from the lighted hallway. Her footfall never woke Dawn's mother. The nurse eased a syringe into Dawn's IV line, and in minutes, darkness overtook her once again.

"That friend of yours—Rhonda—is really persistent." Those were the first words out of Rob's mouth when he came to Dawn's room early the next morning on his way to work. "She's called the house a dozen times and is now in the waiting room trying to finagle her way in here."

Dawn must have managed an expression that communicated her alarm, because Rob shook his head and took her right hand in his. "Don't worry. No one's going to let her in. I know you don't want her seeing you like this."

Dawn squeezed his hand, hoping to let him know that he was absolutely correct. She didn't want anyone seeing her half-paralyzed and unable to talk.

"I told her Katie would call her the minute we know something. I guess she's taken it upon herself to become the spokesperson on your behalf at Hardy High."

Dawn cringed inwardly.

"People are worried about you, Squirt. You've got an amazing number of friends and people who care."

People who are weirdly interested, Dawn thought. She could almost hear the hallway buzz at school. *"Did you hear? That Dawn Rochelle girl passed out in the cafeteria yesterday and had to be taken away in an ambulance."*

"Who?"

"You know—Dawn, that cancer girl."

"Oh—her."

Dawn shuddered. She wanted to be well again before she saw anybody from school. Even Rhonda. Then she felt guilty. Rhonda had been her friend for years. Maybe when Dawn felt better, she'd allow Rhonda to visit.

"Mom's gone home to shower and change." Rob interrupted Dawn's thoughts. "And Katie will be here right after lunch. The neighbor's watching Keegan again. And as soon as the workday's over, I'll be back." He leaned down and kissed her forehead. "We're going to get through this. You're going to beat this thing just like you've beaten cancer."

She longed for his words to be prophetic. What

was happening to her wasn't fair! She'd paid her dues to sickness and disease already. A stroke—something that generally happened to older people—just wasn't fair!

Once Rob was gone, Dawn realized that she was alone in the room, and until her mother returned, she would remain alone. She looked for the TV remote and saw that it was dangling by its cord outside the rail on the left side of the bed. Her left side was useless. She tried to pull herself over with her right hand, but half her body felt like a dead weight. Suddenly she realized just how helpless she was. She could reach nothing—not her bedside stand, not the water pitcher, not even the TV remote.

She considered pressing the call button for a nurse, then realized she couldn't reach that, either. And when she tried to raise the head of the hospital bed with the buttons she could reach, she started to slide down the bed. Her feet didn't touch the foot, so she couldn't even brace herself. She was helpless, powerless to do even the simplest task for herself. Cold sweat broke out all over her, and she shivered. She told herself not to cry but couldn't stem the trickle of tears that ran down her cheeks. She blotted her face on the bedsheet with her good hand.

For the time being, she was stuck, and until

someone came into the room to help her, there was nothing more to do except weep and pray that this nightmare called *stroke* would magically end and set her free to get back on track with her life.

It took two days for the paralysis to stop spreading. After another EEG (a printout that showed electrical activity in her brain), a second CAT scan, and an echocardiogram of her heart, Dr. Weinstein had some answers for Dawn and her family.

He sat them down in Dawn's room, a heavy stack of paperwork in his hands. "You've had a brain attack, an ischemic stroke," he began. "A fifty-cent word that means the blood supply inside your brain got cut off. It can be congenital— you're born with malformed vessels that one day clog on you." He paused. "Or it can be caused by some outside factor—in your case, perhaps all the chemo you received when you had your leukemia."

"But that's not fair!" Dawn's mother erupted. "She *had* to have the chemo. There was no choice, and certainly no mention of a stroke possibility."

"Dawn went through chemo with drugs we don't even use anymore," Dr. Weinstein said. "Treatment's come a long way in the years since

33

her original diagnosis. But it doesn't matter. She would have died without the chemo."

"Cold comfort," Rob growled.

"What's important is that we deal with what's happening now." Dr. Weinstein looked directly at Dawn. "Your particular clot formed deep within the right side of your brain. Too deep for surgery."

Brain surgery! Dawn could hardly believe her ears. She didn't want to undergo an operation on her brain. She didn't want doctors opening up her head and poking around. Even when she'd had leukemia, doctors hadn't cut open her body. She heard her parents gasp, so she knew they were put off by the idea too.

"You said the right side of her brain," Dawn's father said. "But she can't move the left side of her body."

"It's the way the brain works. The nerves cross over from the right side of the brain to control the left side of the body and vice versa. Some of the right-brain functions include memory, speech, and swallowing. That's why it's difficult for you to speak or eat. That's why all your food is puréed—to keep you from choking."

She hated the mushed-up food she was being served. It looked like Keegan's baby food. She wasn't hungry anyway, so it was easy to not eat.

Not being able to talk was worse. She wondered, *Will I ever speak again?*

"The good news is that we believe the worst is over for you. The paralysis has stopped advancing. Now it's a matter of recovery."

"When can Dawn go home?" Rob asked.

"I'll move her over to the rehab unit across the street first, probably in another week. We won't release her to go home until we know she can navigate on her own."

What a joke! Dawn thought. She couldn't even get out of bed without help. The nurses had to put her into a wheelchair and roll her down the hall to the shower room so that she could be bathed. Her mother took care of helping her brush her teeth and comb her hair. Even in her worst days of chemo, Dawn had never been so helpless and dependent. Not since she was a toddler had someone had to help feed her. True, her right side worked, but it took so much mental concentration for her to do even the smallest tasks that Dawn wearied easily.

Dr. Weinstein stood up. "You haven't had any more seizures, and that's good news. You won't have to take anticonvulsants. You're young, Dawn. It's going to take some hard work on your part, but I think you'll come back strong."

She wanted to believe him, but when a

person's body refused to obey the simple commands of her brain, how much hope did she really have of winning her battle? Dawn watched him leave the room and envied his simple ability to do so.

"It may be a long haul, Squirt, but you can do it," she heard Rob say.

"We'll help every way we can," her mother assured her.

"We love you, Dawn," her father added.

She felt grateful to them but couldn't stop wondering just how long a "haul" her recovery would be. Moreover, would she recover completely? Or would she always carry the telltale signs of her brain attack? And most of all, she wondered, *Can it happen to me again?*

Chapter
Six

After ten days in the main hospital, Dawn was transferred to the hospital's rehabilitation unit across the street. Her new room was spacious and bright, and once again she had no roommate, which suited her just fine.

"I'm Haley Conroy, and I'm going to be one of your physical therapists. While you're here, you'll be working very hard to rebuild strength and stamina. My job is to get you back on your feet as soon as possible." The woman speaking to Dawn looked to be in her early twenties, with shoulder-length dark hair, pulled back into a ponytail. Dawn also noticed that she didn't exactly walk into the room—she bounced in. Dawn found Haley's energy daunting.

"Hello." Dawn's voice was returning, although she had trouble recognizing it as hers with its monotonous quality. Another problem was that often she knew what she wanted to say but couldn't get it out. At other times she couldn't even come up with the words she wanted to use. Both extremes were so frustrating that she was frequently brought to the brink of tears.

"We're off to rehab," Haley said, scooting a wheelchair alongside Dawn's bed.

"I'll come with you," Dawn's mother said.

"Not this time," Haley told her. "She'll do better if she's concentrating and not distracted by an audience. I'll bring her back after her workout."

The rehab room was brightly lit and reminded Dawn of a gym. Sunlight streamed through banks of windows, and Dawn saw that the trees outside were brilliant with autumn leaves. Sadly she realized that time was passing her by while she was stuck in this no-man's-land of hospital life, just as she had been when she was thirteen. Except then she'd had Sandy for a friend, a girl like her, who suffered from leukemia. Now Dawn was surrounded by elderly people and physically fit therapists.

Haley pushed Dawn's wheelchair through the space, pointing out apparatuses that looked as elementary as enormous rubber beach balls and as complicated as equipment used by dedicated body builders. "We have a pool in there,"—she pointed at a closed door—"and you'll do hydrotherapy three times a week. You'll learn how to stand and walk all over again." Haley stopped in front of a set of parallel bars with a nonskid rubber mat running between them. She locked the wheels on the chair and dragged a walker in front of Dawn.

"I'm going to help you up. Later I'll put you between the bars. Let's see how well you can stand."

Panic seized Dawn. She wasn't ready. She'd fall down. "Can't," she whispered.

"I won't let you fall," Haley said. "I'm strong." She posed like a muscleman to make her point. "Now come on. You don't want to be stuck in that chair forever, do you?"

With Haley's help, Dawn got out of the chair, and as Haley shouldered the full weight of Dawn's left side, Dawn grabbed hold of the walker with her right hand. She was upright! Out of bed, out of a wheelchair, and fully upright! "I—I'm standing." Her words were labored, but a sense of accomplishment surged through Dawn.

"And soon you'll be walking, and after that dancing. Did you ever take ballet lessons?"

"No."

"I did. I wanted to be a ballerina in the worst way, but I was too short. Ballerinas are very tall and elegant, you know." Haley paused, eased Dawn back into the wheelchair. She looked down at her and asked, "What do you want, Dawn?"

Dawn worked hard to form the phrase in her mind, then harder still to get out the words. Finally she said, "I want to be whole again."

Over the next few days, Dawn saw numerous therapists, but Haley soon became her favorite. Haley encouraged, cajoled, joked, and teased Dawn into cooperating, even when Dawn was certain she couldn't perform the task Haley asked of her. Dawn's left hand remained useless, but Haley gave her a range of motor exercises to do by herself. Dawn was to lift her left arm with her right hand, stretching and rotating it to keep it limber. Dawn was thankful that her right hand worked, and at Haley's urging, she took over brushing her own teeth and hair and even learned how to put on makeup.

An occupational therapist named Melissa made Dawn a hand and wrist brace and worked her left hand to keep the joints limber and muscles pliable. At times a feeling like pins and needles invaded Dawn's arm, as if it had gone to sleep. At other times she couldn't feel it at all. Melissa taught Dawn how to do weight-bearing exercises, such as leaning against a table with her left hand, and how to use therapy putty—a pliable clay that she squeezed and pinched to rebuild strength and dexterity.

Words still came hard. The first day the speech therapist, Linda, gave her a book to read, Dawn only stared at the cover in dismay.

"It's a baby book," Dawn said with effort, and tossed it onto the table in Linda's office.

"A stroke victim often has to take baby steps before she can take big steps." Linda slid the book back to Dawn.

With disdain, Dawn opened it and stared down at a picture of a small child holding a balloon. To her horror, she couldn't see the left page of the book at all. Stricken, she looked up. "I—I can't see. . . . What's wrong with me?"

"Don't be alarmed," Linda said. "It's probably left visual neglect. It happens frequently in stroke victims." Linda moved the book toward the right, and the page popped into focus.

Dawn began to tremble. If she couldn't see to read, how was she ever going to finish high school? "Will it go away?"

"It usually does."

Tears welled in Dawn's eyes, making the letters squiggle. "I-it's hard to focus. And the letters . . ." She blinked. "I—I can't read all the letters." Some of the letters looked strange, and she couldn't recall what they were.

"It won't take long for you to retrain your memory cells to make up for the ones you've lost,

Dawn," Linda said kindly. "We just have to rewire some of your circuitry. Once you dig in, it'll come back fast."

Rewire. That's what all the therapists were trying to help her do. The stroke had destroyed millions of brain cells, and once brain cells died they could never be regenerated. Other cells had to be trained to take up the slack. Yet the tasks before Dawn seemed overwhelming, like a mountain too tall to climb. How could she possibly rewire—relearn in months what it had taken her seventeen years to acquire? She couldn't. It was impossible.

That night a hard look in the mirror told Dawn the truth; she was a freak. Her left eyelid drooped, her left arm and hand were red and swollen to twice their normal size. Besides her appearance, her brain couldn't decipher simple symbols. No amount of physical therapy was going to erase the marks of her stroke. Anyone who paused to look at her would know something was wrong with her. Life as she had known it was over.

"You're depressed, Dawn. I can see that. Dr. Weinstein said it could happen." Dawn's mother was sitting across from her at a table in the corner of her room, eating dinner. Her mother had taken to having hospital meals delivered for herself so that the two of them could eat together.

"Good call, Mom." Dawn toyed with her food, no longer puréed but cut into a child's bite-size pieces that she had to chase around her plate with a fork. "I still have to have my mommy . . . c-cut up my food."

"I'm not going to tell you to not be depressed. You have plenty to be depressed about. But you're alive. That's what really counts."

You call this living? Dawn wanted to yell, but of course the words got all tangled in her head and she ended up making a guttural sound, like some cornered animal.

"All right. Maybe this is a good time to show you some things." Her mother stood, marched over to the closet, opened it, and drew out a cardboard box. She pushed Dawn's tray aside and dumped the box. Piles of unopened letters spilled out. "We've been saving these for you. They're from your friends, family from out of town, even strangers who've heard what happened to you. More mail arrives daily at home. People are concerned, Dawn. They want you to get well. Poor Rhonda is frantic to come visit you."

Dawn shook her head. "No."

Her mother sighed. "Will you at least look at some of this mail? I know it will cheer you up."

Dawn fingered a few of the envelopes. "Why have . . . you . . . saved . . . them?"

"We thought it would be best, that's all."

Dawn knew the truth her mother wasn't telling her. They had saved them because they knew she couldn't read them.

"Can I open one for you?"

Dawn shrugged. It was too difficult to express her anger and frustration. Besides, her mother was going to do whatever she wanted to do, with or without Dawn's permission.

Her mother picked up a red envelope and studied the postmark. "This one arrived two weeks ago." She slipped her dinner knife beneath the flap and sliced through the colorful paper. She pulled out a card and set it on the table in front of Dawn. "I'm going for a walk down the hall so that you can look at your mail in private."

Once Dawn was alone, several minutes passed before she worked up the courage to turn the card over. On the front was a picture of an old-fashioned teddy bear. Mist swam before her eyes. When she'd been a little girl, she'd loved teddy bears. Her favorite, Mr. Ruggers, had gone every-place with her, even to the hospital when she'd been thirteen. Slowly Dawn used her right hand to open the card. The printed words inside all ran together and she had to hold it toward her right side to focus. She couldn't make sense of the message. Still, at the bottom, in bold black letters, was a signature. "J-a-k-e." She sounded out the word. *Jake*.

He had sent her a card when she'd been in the hospital with leukemia, and it, too, had shown a drawing of a teddy bear. He had remembered after all these years that she liked teddy bears. She knew she should be happy and feel warm and fuzzy all over. But all she felt was sadness—a deep, dark well of sadness for all that she had lost. For all that she might never have again.

Chapter
Seven
❧ ❧

"You're not trying, Dawn. Don't tell me you've given up already?" Haley cajoled as Dawn stood between the parallel bars, unable to slide her left foot forward.

"I'm trying," Dawn said. "I—I can't."

A wide black nylon strap helped hold Dawn upright, but her left arm hung limp at her side, and her left leg felt stiff and uncooperative.

"The leg brace is temporary," Haley said, obviously assuming that the contraption on Dawn's leg might be the source of her insecurity. "Your leg will get stronger; then you can lose the brace."

But it wasn't the brace that hampered Dawn. She'd been at the rehab hospital a month, doing intense physical therapy. She'd made progress, especially with reading and speaking, but she couldn't shake her feelings of sadness and aloneness. The rehab center worked with other patients, but they were all old. She was the only person her age working to overcome the effects of her stroke. Sometimes the elderly people stared at her as if they couldn't quite believe their eyes.

"Don't you want to go home?" Haley asked. "Your doctor won't send you home unless you're further along with your therapy."

Dawn wasn't sure how to answer. There in the hospital, she at least felt safe. At home she would be facing the real world—a place she couldn't navigate on her own. "It's better here for me," she told Haley.

"You can't stay here forever. And believe me, you'll be coming often for therapy. It's not as if you'll be abandoned."

Dawn knew that was true, but still the thought of going home unnerved her. What would she do if her friends stopped by to see her? She wasn't ready to face them. While she was in the hospital, she could keep them out. At home she had no such control. Nor was she ready to return to school. She'd already had nightmares about staggering down the halls, people making way for her, stepping aside in horror, pointing and staring. The mail had slackened, but Rhonda called often. Dawn had allowed herself to speak to Rhonda on the phone, mostly because she owed it to the one friend who'd stuck by her all these years.

"I can't believe I'm actually talking to you," Rhonda had squealed the first time Dawn had called. "Oh my gosh! I thought you were mad at me."

"No. Talking's not easy for me."

"That's what your mom told me. But you sound the same to me. Just slower."

"Tell me about school." Dawn had rehearsed the phrase several times, knowing that once Rhonda started talking, Dawn wouldn't have to put out much effort. She was rewarded when Rhonda dove into a long dialogue about the world Dawn had left behind so suddenly.

"Dawn, are you listening to me?" Haley's question jerked Dawn back into her therapy session.

"Yes."

"Progress can be slow. I know that's frustrating. But I'm telling you, hard work now will pay off. Often it takes up to six months for a person to regain mobility. Stroke patients can continue to improve for up to two years."

"What if they don't? What if I don't?"

"We won't know if you stop trying, will we?"

"I've missed . . ." Words darted out of Dawn's mind. She gritted her teeth and tried again.

48

"I've missed . . . a lot of school. How can I ever catch up?"

"One day at a time," Haley told her. "One step at a time. Now, come on. You've got work to do. Let's do it."

"Later," Dawn said, rubbing her eyes. "I'm tired. Want to go back to my . . . room." The leg brace clunked on the side of the wheelchair as she sat down and stared at the floor. Then she looked up and started laughing uncontrollably.

Dr. Weinstein sent a shrink to talk to Dawn. Dr. Grace Baluchia was a psychologist, a pleasant woman about Dawn's mother's age. Dawn felt no motivation to spill her guts to the woman.

"The good news," Dr. Baluchia said, "is that sudden outbursts of uncontrolled emotion are normal for some stroke victims. You can begin to laugh or cry for no reason."

This is supposed to make me feel better? People didn't just burst into tears or laughter for no reason. "I . . . I hate . . . it."

"It will get better."

"I start crying when I don't want to cry."

"These emotional fluctuations are simply part of your recovery process. Think of it as a sneeze that comes on suddenly. You wouldn't be ashamed of sneezing, would you?"

"It . . . still . . . s-stinks."

Dr. Baluchia smiled. "I agree. When it happens, remember that you've had a lot of adjustments to make lately. But all your therapists agree that you're making good progress. Haley's a little concerned because she thinks you've backed off. She thinks you're not trying as hard as you were in the beginning. Is that true?"

Why try? Dawn thought. She was hopelessly behind in school. How could she ever catch up? "It's taking . . . forever," she said in a halfhearted defense.

"Why not set little goals for yourself? Why not concentrate on what you can do instead of what you can't do?"

"I . . . can't do . . . anything." Dawn lifted her left arm and let it plop into her lap to make her point. How could her hand, once so much a part of her functioning body, now be so useless? It felt dead, and she couldn't control it.

"You can read. Linda tells me you've made excellent progress with your language skills."

"Not enough."

"Everything worth doing is difficult. You're on the road to recovery. None of us want you to get sidetracked."

50

Dawn stared over the counselor's head. She didn't want a pep talk or a lecture. How could anyone understand what she was experiencing unless that person had had a stroke? All the therapists in the world couldn't change what Dawn was going through. This stroke was hers and hers alone. She was broken, damaged. Like Humpty Dumpty. How was she ever going to be put back together again?

Dawn dreamed that she was running through a field of flowers. Her arms and legs worked fine, and the feel of the fresh air against her face made her want to whirl and dance and sing. The sound of her own laughter woke her up, and she discovered that she was breathing hard and still lying in her hospital bed. The halls were quiet, the door of her room shut. Her mother no longer spent nights with Dawn. She would come in the morning, leave after lunch, return in time for dinner. Rob, Katie, and Dawn's father visited frequently, more so on weekends.

Dawn sighed, willing herself back to the beautiful sunlit field of her dreams. The image refused to return. Her dimly lit room dissolved through tears, as if the walls were melting. Soon her bed would become a boat and she'd float away.

"So are you just giving up, Dawn Rochelle?"

The question, spoken aloud in a girl's voice, so startled Dawn that she raised the head of her bed to locate the speaker. "Who's there?"

"Don't you recognize me? Gee, thanks a lot!"

In the dimness, Dawn made out the shape of a young girl. Dawn flipped on the bedside light and the girl stepped forward. Dawn's heart almost stopped. "S-Sandy?"

The thirteen-year-old girl smiled. "Aw, so you *do* recognize me. I'm glad."

"But you're, you're . . . ," Dawn couldn't get out the word *dead.*

"Gone, but not forgotten," Sandy said, her face lighting up with a smile. "Anyway, I hope not."

"I'm dreaming, aren't I?"

"Why do you think that? Can't I come visit an old friend if I want?"

"I wish you could." Dawn's voice trembled.

"I'm here now, but not to tell you I feel sorry for you, if that's what you're thinking. I'm here to tell you to get your butt in gear."

"You don't know what it's like. How hard it is."

"Really?" Sandy crossed her arms. "We went through cancer together. I believe I know what's hard."

"I thought it was over for me. You know, the bad times."

"Guess not. But don't be a slacker. You can lick

this thing. I know you can because you licked leukemia—something I couldn't do."

Dawn felt a heaviness in her heart. "I've missed you every day."

"Then do me a favor. Grow up. Get old. Go after Jake. Don't let that Tasha take him away from you."

"How do you know about her?"

"I know a lot of things. Most of all, I know you're no quitter. You weren't when I knew you, anyway."

"I'm not quitting."

Sandy grinned. "Good, then go back to sleep. Tomorrow you can really get to work." She stepped back into the shadows.

"Wait. Don't go. Talk to me some more."

"Talk to your other friends. They miss you too."

The room grew silent. Dawn could feel her heart pounding, the blood rushing in her temples. She was alone. There was no Sandy.

Chapter Eight

❧~ ~❧

"I don't know what turned you around this past week, Dawn, but I wish I could put it in a jar and give big doses of it to my other patients," Haley said as she handed Dawn a towel to wipe the perspiration from her face.

They had just finished a grueling session, and physically Dawn was exhausted, but mentally she felt better than she had in weeks. "You think I'm improving?"

"Absolutely. But it's your attitude that's improved most of all. What happened?"

"I had a visit . . . from an old friend."

"I didn't know you were seeing your friends again. That's wonderful."

"Not that kind of visit. It was in a dream." Dawn had lain awake for hours before finally deciding that her encounter with Sandy had been a dream within a dream. First the field of freedom, then the reality of the hospital room. Both had been parts of the same dream. She realized it because in her conversation with Sandy, Dawn hadn't stammered or fumbled once for a word, hadn't fallen prey to any of the difficulties of speech and thought she experienced from day to day. What she had encountered in the dream was the deepest wish from the bottom of her heart— to be normal, to have her life back. She didn't need a psychologist to tell her that Sandy's appearance had simply been an expression of her need to motivate herself, to give herself the push she needed to fight.

Haley shrugged. "Whatever. It made all the difference. You keep up the good work, and we'll take your field trip next week."

"What field trip?"

"Before they're discharged, stroke patients are taken on an outing in order to help them adjust to life in the real world again."

Dawn recoiled slightly. "Can't the real world wait?"

Haley shook her head. "Nope. We want to take you out in it and let you navigate on your own. Don't worry. I'll be right by your side the whole time."

Dawn swallowed hard. She wasn't sure about

this. She'd thought she'd simply be sent home and would eventually get around to going outside. "Are you sure I have to go?"

"Every patient does it."

"Where will . . . we . . . go?" Whenever she was nervous, she had more difficulty with her speech.

Haley beamed at her. "Why, to the mall, of course."

Dawn's palms sweated during the drive to the mall on Friday morning. She rode with two other patients facing discharge, a seventy-five-year-old man and a sixty-eight-year-old woman, along with their therapists. Dawn gazed out the window, amazed at the crisp, cool autumn weather. When she'd gone into the hospital, the leaves had been turning. Now the branches were bare, prepared for a long winter's sleep. She felt as if *she'd* been in hibernation.

She wore jeans and a sweater and bright white sneakers. Those white shoes would never have found their way into her closet before the stroke. But they had special nonskid soles, so she wore them, because the last thing she wanted to do was lose her balance and end up in a heap. She also wore a leg brace and carried a metal crutch that encircled her right arm to give her balance and support. The van unloaded the group at a side entrance, and the driver said he'd return in an hour to pick them up. Her heart pounding, Dawn wobbled through the sliding automatic door meant for the disabled and into the huge shopping mall she'd cruised countless times with Rhonda and her other friends.

"Where to?" Haley asked. "Any special store you want to check out?"

"Can we just walk around?"

"Sure."

"I'm slow."

"I'm in no hurry."

They set off, with Dawn laboring to coordinate her gait. Once she found her stride, she actually glanced into store windows. Bright displays featured Thanksgiving themes, making her realize all over again how much time she'd spent adjusting to her stroke. "Do you think they'll send me home before Thanksgiving?"

"Yes, I do. Are you looking forward to going home?"

"In some ways. In others, it's scary."

"I know, but I'll be working with you, and so will Katie."

"That's what she told me."

"You're going to do fine, Dawn. Look how far you've come already."

Dawn caught her reflection in a row of mirrored

tiles lining the doorway of a store. She thought she looked odd, like a broken doll someone hadn't quite put back together correctly. She was thin, as she'd been after her initial rounds of chemo. Her jeans hid the leg brace, but her left arm still hung almost useless at her side, and the left side of her face had an eerie, masklike quality. A tear trickled down her cheek. She begged herself not to break into a crying fit. "My eye's leaking."

Haley dabbed at the moisture with a tissue. "Probably the change from the outside to the inside air. I think you're fine now."

Dawn dipped her head, heard laughter, and looked up in time to see a group of girls from her school with their backs to her. She froze. What were they doing here? Why weren't they in class?

"What's wrong?" Haley asked.

"C-Can we go sit down?"

"You all right?"

"Yes, I just need to go . . . some other . . . way." Dawn's mind fogged. She struggled to turn around, pleading silently for the girls not to see her.

"You know those girls?"

"Yes . . . don't want . . . them to see . . . me."

"No problem. Turn left and we'll hit the food court."

When they reached a table, Dawn all but collapsed into a chair, gasping for breath.

"Don't panic," Haley said. "I'll buy us a soda."

Dawn tried to make herself small but felt as if a neon sign were blinking over her head: *Over here! Look at the weirdo!*

Haley returned with sodas. Dawn struggled with the paper straw, gave up, and threw it on the floor in frustration. "I—I can't. . . ."

Haley slipped another straw through the lid of the cup. "Take a sip, slow your breathing. No one saw you. Everything's fine."

Dawn did as she was told, but there was no way she could really tell Haley how *not* fine everything was to her. She'd almost tripped over girls from her class in the mall. It would have been a disaster. She didn't want them to see her. She didn't want anyone to see her. Not until she was better, until she could walk and talk like before.

"I know it's difficult, Dawn, but you're really doing remarkably well. You've come so far. Don't let this set you back."

Dawn nodded, unable to speak because the words and emotions were mixing up in her brain and making her feel light-headed. How much longer was this nightmare going to last?

"Mom, tell Rhonda I want to see her." Dawn was back in the safety of her rehab hospital room that night when she told her mother what she wanted.

"Really? Oh, she'll be so happy. I can't tell you how often I talk to that girl."

On Saturday morning Dawn got up early, showered, and took extra pains with her grooming. Her mother helped blow-dry her hair, then brushed it until it gleamed. Dawn put on makeup and dressed in jeans and a bright green sweater—her best color. She positioned herself in a chair at a table in the visitors' lounge. A TV set along one wall showed cartoons, but Dawn faced the doorway, ignoring the noise, and waited for Rhonda's entrance.

Around eleven Rhonda rushed into the room, spied Dawn, and skidded to a halt.

"Hey, Rhonda," Dawn said, holding her head high.

Tears shimmered in Rhonda's large and luminous eyes. She cupped her hand across her mouth.

"Don't you have anything to say to me?" Dawn felt a momentary wave of panic. She'd worked hard to look as normal as possible. Had she failed so miserably that Rhonda, the nonstop talker, had nothing to say?

Rhonda nodded. She dropped her hand and took a step closer, tears dancing on her lashes. "Um . . ." She cleared her throat. "You have hair," she said.

Chapter
Nine

❧ ❧

"'You have hair'?" Dawn repeated. "I haven't seen you . . . in weeks . . . and all you say is 'You have hair'?"

Rhonda wrung her hands. "Uh . . . lots of hair."

As the absurdity of the scene struck her, Dawn began to laugh. Why, Rhonda was as nervous as she was! "Yes . . . I . . . have hair," she said. "Strokes don't make your hair fall out, girlfriend."

Then suddenly Rhonda bounded toward her, dropped to her knees, and threw her arms around Dawn. She broke into sobs, half laughing, half crying. "That was such a dumb thing to say," she sputtered. "What was I thinking? No chemo with a stroke! I know that."

Dawn took a breath. "No . . . it's my fault . . . making you stay away for so long."

Rhonda rocked back on her heels. "You bet it

was!" She gave Dawn a gentle slap on her arm. "It was very rude of you. I'm supposed to be your best friend, and you wouldn't even let me come see you."

Dawn sobered and looked straight into Rhonda's face. "I didn't want you . . . to see me . . . like this."

"Like how? You look all right to me."

"Not all right." Still self-conscious about her droopy left eyelid, useless left arm, and often monotonous voice, Dawn figured Rhonda was trying to spare her feelings. She'd looked into mirrors; she knew how she looked and how she sounded.

"Of course, you're not *all right*, all right," Rhonda said. "But you're more all right than not all right. Know what I mean?"

"I've got . . . long way to go."

"Are you coming back to school?"

"No. I don't want . . . people staring."

"Oh, like they don't stare at everybody."

"I'm slow."

Rhonda averted her gaze. "I miss you at school."

"No new boys for you?" Dawn switched to one of Rhonda's favorite subjects.

"No new *nothing* for me. Without you, there's no one to really hang with." Rhonda sat cross-legged on the floor.

In the background a cartoon character ran over another character with a steamroller, flattening him. In the next frame the squished character sprang back in perfect condition. *If only it were that easy,* Dawn thought. "How is school?"

"Did I tell you about the Halloween carnival when we talked on the phone?"

"A little."

"We raised money for band uniforms and cheerleading outfits." Rhonda rolled her eyes. "Whoopee. Did I tell you both groups have been invited to Florida to march in some parade at Disney World over Christmas break?"

Dawn shook her head. "Lucky band."

"It's the cheerleaders that drive me crazy—you know, Tasha and her crowd. They really think they're hot stuff. She's no Snow White." Rhonda cut her eyes sideways. "She's after Jake majorly."

Dawn flinched. "Free country."

"He asks me about you all the time. He said he sent you get-well cards. Did he?"

Dawn had three from Jake, and she treasured them. "He feels sorry for me."

"What's wrong with that? I wish some guy felt sorry enough for me to ask my friends about me and send me cards." Rhonda tipped her chin. "You really don't believe he could actually *like* you, do you?"

"Maybe he did . . . once. But now . . ." She didn't finish the sentence.

"Now you have to make a comeback."

Dawn regarded her friend quietly, thinking that to Rhonda it all seemed so simple and uncomplicated. Rhonda had no idea how helpless Dawn felt, how betrayed she felt by her own body and mind. Often the simplest activities overwhelmed her and made her feel stupid and scattered. "No time for boyfriends," Dawn said. "Need to get well . . . to get one hundred percent."

"How long's that going to take?" Rhonda looked perplexed, as if it were an act of will instead of hard, frustrating, and exhausting work.

"Don't know . . . maybe the rest of my life."

Dr. Weinstein released Dawn from the rehab center two days before Thanksgiving. Her mother drove her home along with Dawn's accumulation of things from her hospital stay—boxes of cards, clothes, and stuffed animals. She also had lists and schedules for rehab visits and homebound exercises, and a leg brace and wrist brace for her hand and wrist. Her hand gave her problems, the feeling coming and going on a whim. She was still wobbly when she walked, but she could walk, so there was no need for a wheelchair.

Her mother parked in the garage and helped Dawn from the car. Dawn walked through the door and was greeted by her entire family. Balloons and a Welcome Home banner filled the family room. Her mother had made a chocolate cake, Dawn's favorite. Everyone hugged her. Keegan gurgled and gave her a toothy grin. "He's grown so much," Dawn said, feeling tears slide down her cheeks in spite of trying hard not to cry.

"We fixed up the sun porch for you," Rob said. "Come see."

They moved to the room off the kitchen. The antique wicker furniture had been crammed into one end, and an electric floor heater made the room toasty warm. Several pieces of new gym equipment shone in the afternoon sunlight coming through the windows.

"Now you can work out anytime you want," Katie said. "You'll have your strength back in no time."

"I—I don't know what to say."

"I do the treadmill myself," her mother said. "I've already lost five pounds."

"How about my room?" Dawn had worried about making it up the stairs for days. "Should I sleep down here?"

"Come see," her father said. "We tried to think of everything."

In the foyer, next to the stairs, Dawn saw a boxlike contraption. "Is that a . . ." The word she wanted suddenly fled, and no matter how hard she tried, she couldn't find it.

"It's an elevator, all right," her father said, as if filling in a blank for her.

"For me?"

"Well, your mom and I aren't getting any younger, so it seemed like a good investment for us, too."

He could say what he liked, but Dawn knew they'd put in an expensive elevator for her sake.

"Try it out, Squirt," Rob said, pulling open the door.

Inside, the elevator was brightly lit but small. "Can it hold both of us?"

"Up to five hundred pounds," Rob said with a grin. "Come on, Keegan, let's take your aunt for a ride." He took the baby from Katie and stepped into the elevator. Dawn followed. Rob closed the door, which had a clear half-panel that kept her from feeling claustrophobic, and pushed the Up button. The elevator gears hummed, and slowly the elevator rose.

Dawn grinned as the floor below dropped away. Her mom waved. "I feel silly," Dawn said.

"They only did it because they love you," Rob said.

"I know."

The elevator stopped, and Rob slid open the door. Katie, who had come up the stairs, was waiting for them. "It's not the fastest means of transportation, but it gets the job done."

Dawn hobbled to her room and stood in the doorway. Overcome with emotion, she remembered coming home from the hospital when she'd been thirteen. Her bed had been lined with teddy bears then, the wallpaper trimmed with a teddy bear border print. The room was now a sunny yellow, the bedspread white eyelet.

At thirteen, she had been racked by leukemia, weakened by chemo. Now she was seventeen, the victim of a "brain attack," and her body looked like that of an arthritic old woman.

But she was home. Home, with a family who loved her, who had always stood by her, who was willing to do anything to help make her life better, easier. She knew she couldn't let them down, no matter how long her recovery took or how much it hurt.

Chapter
Ten
❧ ～ ❧

On Thanksgiving morning, Dawn woke to the mingling aromas of roasting turkey and spicy pumpkin pies. She made her way down the hall to the bathroom and showered, careful to use the special grab bars her father had installed, thinking back to the time before her stroke, when she breezed through her morning routine without a second thought. Now everything she did took her twice as long. When she was finally dressed and ready, she rode the elevator down and went into the kitchen.

"Hey, sleepyhead," Katie called cheerfully. She was chopping celery while Dawn's mother peeled carrots for her famous carrot salad, which she only served on holidays. Keegan sat in his high chair gnawing on a cookie. He offered Dawn a gooey-faced smile.

"Can I do anything?" Dawn asked, knowing that usually she was the one helping her mother prepare the big meal.

"You could peel potatoes," her mother started. Then, glancing at Dawn's still useless left hand, she added, "Um—no, I think we have it all under control."

"Maybe I could set the table."

"I've asked Rob—"

"Don't you think I can do it?"

"Of course you can do it," her mother said.

"Then let me try."

Agitated, and piqued at her mother, Dawn retreated to the dining room and saw that a clean white cloth had already been spread across the table. A vase of fall flowers and a cluster of colorful gourds were arranged as the centerpiece. She hobbled to the hutch and removed a plate, returned to the table, and set it down. *One down,* she told herself, then began the process all over again. The work was laborious and taxing, but she did it all, from the plates to the full place settings of her mother's good silver and fine crystal goblets. She was concentrating so hard that she didn't realize Rob was watching her from the doorway until she was finished.

"Slow, huh?" she said, flushing.

"But a good job. Thanks."

"For what? Keegan could have done it faster."

"Thanks because I was supposed to do it and I can't ever remember what fork goes where."

"I'll draw you a . . ." The word she wanted fled her memory.

Rob waited a few seconds before asking, "A diagram? Is that what you wanted to say?"

"I hate when I forget."

"Lighten up on yourself. Lapses are to be expected."

She brushed past him and limped into the family room. She didn't want anybody's pity, especially her brother's. Sitting on the sofa in a funk, she heard the doorbell ring and heard Rob go to the door. Minutes later he came into the room and said, "There's someone here to see you."

Startled, Dawn looked up. Rhonda was out of town for the holiday. "I don't want to see anyone."

"Not even me?" It was Jake Macka who asked the question.

Her heart lurched, and she felt sick to her stomach. Her gaze was pulled toward him like metal to a magnet. He wore jeans and his football jacket, his hands jammed into the pockets.

"I guess I'll go help Dad in the garage," Rob said, retreating.

If she could have moved fast enough, she

would have grabbed Rob's arm and told him to stay. She was furious with him. He knew how she felt about visitors. But Rob was gone, and she was alone in the room with dark-haired, brown-eyed Jake.

"Can I sit?" he asked.

"You shouldn't have come." Dawn heard the wooden sound of her own voice and hated it.

"I thought about calling first," Jake said, lowering himself into the armchair directly across from the sofa. "But I knew you wouldn't take the call."

She tried to avoid eye contact but couldn't. "Probably . . . not." How could he just show up on her doorstep? Was it morbid curiosity? She knew Rhonda had spread the word that Dawn wanted to be left alone.

Jake leaned forward and took her right hand in his. "Dawn, I don't want to upset you, but I wanted to see you, talk to you. It's been almost two months since we've even spoken. I thought we were friends."

"Things . . . are different . . . now." She felt as if she were falling apart; she couldn't concentrate. Conversation took such an effort, and she didn't want to sound stupid and clumsy to him.

"Why? Because you had a stroke? You had cancer, too, and you beat it."

She felt frozen in place, unable to meet his gaze.

He let go of her hand and moved to get up. "I won't stay. I was just thinking about what I wanted instead of what you wanted. I'm sorry."

"No." The word was out of her mouth before she could stop it. "All right . . . you're here now. This is . . . the new . . . me."

He dipped his head to catch her gaze and smiled when he did. "I think you look great."

She shrugged, not believing him. "Nice of you to say."

"A little skinny, but I know how you girls like being skinny, so I won't tell you to stuff your face with turkey today like I'm going to do."

He was trying hard to ask forgiveness, and she felt petty. She wanted to be near him, and since he'd already seen her, heard her speak, there was no going back. There was no way of ever changing his first impression of her. "Nice jacket."

"Thanks. I'm surprised I even lettered. Thanks to me, we lost the district finals."

"I—I didn't know." During her hospital and rehab stay, Dawn had purposely not asked about the happenings at Hardy High. She had cut herself off because it had been too painful to hear details of all she was missing.

"I missed a field goal in the last game. The ball squirted to the outside and *bam*, it was all over, and instead of advancing to the state play-offs, we were sent packing. Coach was kind about it, but I knew he was really disappointed. That's the closest we've been to state play-offs in six years. Some of the guys really made me feel like a total loser."

"Not very nice."

"Want to know what pulled me out of it?" He didn't wait for her response but said, "You did."

"Me?"

"I kept thinking about you up in that hospital. I'd missed a field goal. You were fighting to get your life back. I read about strokes. I know how bad they can be."

He'd also read about leukemia when she'd had it. Perhaps it was only out of curiosity, but still, it made her feel good that he'd gone to the trouble. "I had a bad one," she said.

"That's what Rhonda told me. I'm really sorry."

"It's over."

"If there's anything you want—I mean, if there's something I can do for you, tell me, all right?"

"Nothing . . . anyone can do . . ." Her voice faltered.

He got to his feet. "I've got to get back home. Mom's putting on a big feast."

"Mine too."

"I hope you're not mad at me for barging in."

Yes, she thought, but she said, "No."

"Can I visit you again sometime?"

She considered his request, still wishing she'd had more time to prepare. She would have put off this reunion for a long, long time. "Not . . . soon."

"Fair enough. And next time I'll call first." He pulled a slightly bent card from his pocket. "It's a Thanksgiving Day card. Corny, huh?"

"Thank you."

At the doorway he turned. "Oh, Tasha said to tell you hello. She's sorry about what happened and hopes you'll be back to school soon."

Not likely, Dawn thought. "No plans yet."

She watched him close the front door behind him, staring for a long time at the space where he'd stood. The smell of turkey, along with the sound of her family laughing together in the kitchen, made her feel more alone than ever. Jake had come to see her. She should be glad. Under normal circumstances, she would have been. But she only felt let down and sad about his visit. The last words he'd spoken had been about Tasha. Life went on. The world of high school—of boyfriends, of football games and hanging out—was for people other than her. Once more, Dawn was an outsider, separated by an event beyond her control.

Chapter
Eleven

"Mom, I want to catch up with my classes." The day after Thanksgiving, Dawn found her mother making out a shopping list at her kitchen desk and delivered her pronouncement. Normally they would have gone off to the mall to get a jump-start on Christmas shopping, but not this year.

Her mother set down her pen. "I'm sure you can go onto the homebound program like you did when you were thirteen. You don't have to push yourself, you know. Is this really what you want?"

"Yes." Dawn had thought about it for days. It wasn't enough to go to rehab for her body to become whole again. She wanted her mind working at one hundred percent too.

Her mother nodded. "I'll call your principal and see what she suggests."

On Monday afternoon Mrs. Gagliano came to the house. The principal of Hardy High was a slight woman with short brown hair and a pretty face, her eyes framed by rimless glasses. She had a habit of standing in the halls between classes, greeting students and addressing them by name, and a reputation for being tough but fair. When she came into the Rochelles' living room, Dawn felt intimidated.

"How are you, Dawn?" Mrs. Gagliano asked, taking the chair across from the sofa where Dawn sat with her mother.

"I'm . . . getting better."

"We've all been pulling for you. Everyone in the school was affected in some way by your diagnosis. I saw girls crying in the bathroom when they first heard about it."

Embarrassed, Dawn didn't know what to say.

"My father had a stroke," the principal added. "He was in his seventies and had clogged arteries. He threw a blood clot and stroked out."

"Did he recover?" Dawn's mother asked.

"Not totally. I only tell you this because I really do understand what you're going through."

"Thank you," Dawn said.

Mrs. Gagliano smiled and leaned forward. "Your mother tells me you want to resume classes."

"Home study," Dawn said.

"Of course. It won't be a problem."

"I—I want . . . to stay up . . . with my class. I want to . . . walk with them . . . in June."

Dawn's mother turned toward her with a surprised look, but the principal's gaze stayed level. "You've missed a whole grading period and part of another."

"I know."

"Catching up won't be easy. Keeping up may prove difficult."

"I thought you might finish up in summer term," her mother said, offering Dawn an easy out.

Dawn shook her head. "I want to try . . . to stay with my class. I still want to . . . go to college."

"And you will," her mother said. "But you don't have to plan so far ahead. You've got plenty of time."

"It's what . . . I want now." Dawn looked straight into her principal's eyes.

"I admire you for your determination," Mrs. Gagliano said. "Before I came today, I checked your scores and grades. You're a top student and very bright. Tell you what: I'll talk to your teachers, see what they think. They'll have to give you assignments and create tests anyway for home study. If they're willing to work with your homebound teacher, you certainly have my permission."

"Thank you."

"Of course, you realize that the homebound program may not be adequate for meeting your goals."

Mrs. Gagliano was being kind in not saying that Dawn's hopes to stay on course and graduate with her class might be unrealistic for someone in her condition. Dawn herself wasn't sure she could do it, but she knew she had to try. The thought of repeating the year, or even a semester, was unacceptable.

"We'll get Dawn a tutor," her mother said. "If she can do the work, she should have the chance of graduating on schedule."

"I agree." Mrs. Gagliano stood and shook Dawn's hand. "But if you catch up, I hope you'll consider returning to classes. You'd be quite an inspiration, and the student body needs an example of what hard work and determination can do. Many of them just coast along instead of really working."

Dawn nodded, but she knew she'd never want to go back to regular classes. At home she could feel safe, and with a tutor it wouldn't matter how slurred her speech became or how long it took her to do an assignment. She felt confident that she could do the work if she took her time. What she could never feel confident about was returning to halls where stares and whispers would follow her everywhere she went.

Rhonda's grandmother gave her a car as an early Christmas gift, and the first week in December Rhonda took Dawn for a ride. They stopped at a hamburger place in a part of the city where they were sure they wouldn't run into anyone from their school. Sitting at the table sipping a shake and eating a burger made Dawn feel more normal than anything she'd done in months.

"Do you like your tutor?" Rhonda asked between bites.

"Her name's Mrs. Appleton, and she teaches part-time at the community college. She's home-schooled four kids. They're all finished with college now, and each one graduated at the top of their class, so I'm hoping she can work the same miracle for me." Dawn took another sip of her shake. Stringing sentences together was getting easier, and besides, she felt more relaxed with Rhonda, less self-conscious about her handicaps.

"Well, I miss you and wish you were back at school."

"I've still got a long way to go."

"Maybe I can come by and she can coach me in geometry. I just don't get it."

"Math is easier than writing for me."

"Really? English used to be your favorite subject."

Dawn's range of vision was improving—a good sign, and more evidence that her hard work in therapy was paying off—but reading was still a struggle. Mrs. Appleton had brought her some recorded books, and they helped. Somehow listening wasn't as hard as concentrating on letters, which squirmed on paper when she stared at them too long. "I know. Mrs. Appleton says it will get easier . . . but some days I wonder."

"I talked to Jake today. He wants to come see you again."

"I'm not ready."

"Well, if you want my advice, I wouldn't shut him out for too long. Plenty of girls would like to have his attention."

"Like Tasha."

"Yes, like Tasha. She makes it a point to be wherever he is but acts as if she just ran into him accidentally. She's so snaky." Rhonda made a face. "And guys are so dense. You'd think he could see through her little schemes."

"Look, you can't blame Tasha for liking Jake."

"Says who?"

Dawn smiled. "You can't be my watchdog for-ever."

"I'm just trying to be a good friend." Rhonda sounded hurt.

Dawn fiddled with her straw and thought hard about how to say what she wanted to say. "You're my *best* friend. But you think that . . . just because I've liked Jake Macka for years, it will work out between us. Like a fairy tale."

"What's wrong with that?"

"It's just that this is real life. And ever since I was thirteen, I've known that real life doesn't usually work out the way I want it to."

"Sometimes I don't like real life. It stinks when your best friend could up and die. So I think she should have a shot at the one guy she's always liked. Maybe I do believe in fairy tales, but so what? In fairy tales people live happily ever after. I like that idea."

"Everything I do these days takes energy, Rhonda. And right now I need all my energy to get well. I don't have time to chase after some fairy tale."

Rhonda gave Dawn a blank stare, and Dawn realized that Rhonda didn't understand her point. But then, how could she? Rhonda had never faced an illness more serious than the flu. Dawn had spent all her teen years doing battle with one malady or another. People who weren't sick, people who'd never been where Dawn had been, just didn't get it. Neither Rhonda nor Jake truly understood this strange and scary fellowship Dawn belonged to—a fellowship of illness in which people lived from day to day and *nobody* lived happily ever after. They simply made the best of whatever life they had left.

Chapter Twelve

Dawn fell into a routine of rehab at the hospital four mornings a week with Haley and two afternoons a week at home with Katie. At her parents' insistence, she took Sundays to relax—as if that were possible. Riding the stationary bike became for her a benchmark of how well she was doing. When she'd first tried it at the rehab center, she couldn't coordinate the pedals or maintain a sustained ride. By Christmas she could ride for thirty minutes.

"Good exercise for your heart," Haley always told her. But whenever Dawn pressed her to say how long it might take to master a new skill, Haley would reply, "How many stars in the sky?" Dawn knew that meant *There's no way to predict the time it might take.*

And for Dawn, time was an enemy. She only

had six months until graduation, and in her opinion, still a very long way to go.

She worked hard for Mrs. Appleton and her homebound teacher, often staying up late into the night to complete assignments, forcing herself to concentrate, memorize, and repeat facts and information aloud. Writing was painstakingly slow, and she had to use a tablet with a weighted back because she couldn't hold down a piece of paper with her left hand while her right hand wrote. Single sheets slid all over the desk, as slippery as eels in oily water. She used her computer whenever possible because typing was easier than writing in longhand. She grew proficient at one-handed typing, though she had to use the same hand to click the mouse.

When school was dismissed for Christmas break, her homebound teacher said, "We'll start again in January."

She begged Mrs. Appleton, her tutor, to keep coming through the holidays.

"My family's coming to visit, but I'll be here the week after Christmas. You have assignments you can do without me, don't you?"

"Two term papers for English." Dawn dreaded tackling them.

"I'll check them over in January. Now, have a *fun* holiday."

As if . . ., Dawn thought.

Many skills eluded Dawn in spite of therapy—washing both hands at the same time, using a curling iron, tying her own sneakers. Some days her left hand seemed better—then progress would stop and her hand would return to its state of uselessness. "My left hand has a mind of its own," she told Rhonda on a day when Rhonda had come over to watch videos and—without warning—Dawn's left hand began to twitch uncontrollably. Just the day before, she'd been able to pick nuts and bolts from the therapy putty for Melissa.

"You mean you're not doing that on purpose?"

"No." Dawn saw instantly that Rhonda was grossed out. She put her right hand atop her left in an effort to stop its movements. "Now do you understand why I don't want to go back to school? Can you imagine how this would go over in the rumor mill?"

"People expect you to be different."

"I don't want to be different. I want to be the way I used to be."

"You will be."

Rhonda eyed Dawn's hand with mistrust, and Dawn regretted her having seen the incident at all. "You—um—won't mention this to anyone, will you?"

"No way. I'm not a traitor. I won't tell anyone anything you don't want me to."

"Thanks," Dawn said, grateful in every way for Rhonda's loyalty.

Three days before Christmas, Jake called and asked if he could stop by in the afternoon to tell her something. Dawn hadn't seen him since Thanksgiving and felt better prepared for a visit, so she told him okay. She spent the morning at rehab, came home, and fell asleep on the sofa. The persistent ringing of the doorbell woke her. When she recalled that her mother had gone Christmas shopping and she was alone, she staggered to the door.

"I thought you'd changed your mind," Jake said.

She felt groggy, and grumbled at herself for going to sleep in the first place. "No . . . I was reading."

He touched her cheek. "Well, you've got big indentations on your face. Must have been a heavy book."

She blushed and rubbed the impression of the sofa cushion with her hand. "Um—come into the living room."

"Nice tree," he said, standing in front of the

tree, which was decorated with white lights, red bows, and silver tinsel she'd hung herself. He took a seat in the chair he'd used at Thanksgiving.

She got comfortable on the sofa. "So, what's up?"

"We leave for Florida tomorrow morning, and I won't be back until after New Year's Day."

"I didn't know you were going to Florida."

"For that parade thing in Orlando. The band and cheerleaders are going. We raised the money last fall."

"Rhonda told me about the parade, but I forgot. And she didn't say you were going."

"Coach asked a few of us players to wear our jerseys and march along with the band. You can watch it on TV on Christmas day. Maybe I'll wave to you." He grinned.

Evidently the coach didn't hold the missed field goal against Jake, since he wanted him to go to Florida. "You mean everybody in the band has to spend Christmas day in Florida?"

"No one minds. Lots of parents are going, and we'll all do Disney World the day after Christmas, plus my folks want to go on down to Miami, too. It'll be okay."

Dawn knew that even if she'd been perfectly healthy, she wouldn't have been a part of the event, which sort of made it better for her. "I hope you have a good time."

"We're all staying at some big hotel together. I can't see myself hanging with some of those band geeks, but Ed's going and so are Rick and Travis."

She remembered the guys from the team—guys she'd seen every day in the halls, the jocks, the important guys—and realized she hadn't thought of them once since her stroke. Her world had grown very small, and high school had become foreign territory.

Jake shuffled his feet. "Also, I want to give you your Christmas present."

She sat up straighter. "You got me a present? I—um—didn't get you anything."

"You weren't supposed to. It's not much, just something I thought you'd like."

He held out a long, brightly wrapped box. "You want to open it now, or do you want me to put it under your tree?"

She knew he wanted her to open it in front of him, but she didn't want to fumble with the wrapping. She'd be clumsy trying to unwrap it with only one hand. "Can I put it under the tree and open it on Christmas day? More presents that way," she added lamely.

"Oh, sure." He stood, but she saw that he was disappointed.

"It's . . . very nice of you . . . thank you . . . really."

"Merry Christmas," he said hastily. "Don't get up. I'll let myself out." From the doorway he said, "Don't forget to watch the parade."

She waited until she heard his car pull off before picking up the box. She pulled and tugged at the ribbon with her hand, then her teeth, until it shredded. She stabbed the thick foil paper with a pencil, ripping the pretty wrapping into strips and wishing she could be less destructive. When the paper fell away at last, she lifted the top off a flat white box and found a thin silver bracelet with a teddy bear charm dangling from it.

She held it up, admired it, wondered how best to wear it. She couldn't put it on by herself around her right wrist, and if she put it on her left wrist, it would sparkle and draw attention to her pathetic left hand. She sat for a few moments, pondering her quandary. She thought of Jake going into the store, choosing this special bracelet just for her. A lump formed in her throat, and she felt ashamed that she hadn't opened his gift while he was there.

With a sigh, she draped the bracelet around

her left wrist and fastened the clasp. She lifted her left arm with her good hand, held it toward the light, and watched the silver bear dance in the rays of the waning sun, a prisoner held in place by a slender silver chain, like a ghost from her own childhood.

Chapter Thirteen

Rhonda came over midmorning on Christmas day, carrying a sackful of presents for Dawn as well as gifts for Keegan.

"Why'd you buy so much for me?" Dawn wanted to know once they'd settled in her room.

"And who else am I going to buy for?"

"But so many!"

"I got carried away. Sue me."

Dawn went to her bedroom closet and brought out a sack heaped with gifts for Rhonda.

"You *dog*," Rhonda squealed. "You got me just as much. When did you go shopping?"

Dawn wiggled the fingers of her right hand. "The Internet and Mom's credit card. Don't worry— I had permission."

They took turns opening each other's gifts. Katie had wrapped Rhonda's for Dawn, and Dawn noted that Rhonda's wrapping of her presents was simple, which she appreciated. Rhonda had mostly slapped colored bows and stickers onto the boxes and had decorated several with felt-tip pens and glitter. They got a huge laugh out of their two "special" gifts for each other—exactly the same sweater, but in different colors.

"I love this!" Rhonda cried, rushing to the mirror beside Dawn's dresser and holding up the fitted striped sweater. "I wanted to keep the one I gave you but knew I had to give it to you 'cause I bought it for you."

Dawn smoothed her hand across the sweater Rhonda had gotten her. "I love mine too. Thanks."

It was then that Rhonda noticed the silver bracelet, and Dawn told her it was from Jake. "I *told* you he liked you," Rhonda crowed. "I love it when I'm right!"

Dawn colored. "It was nice of him. I won't go as far as saying he *likes me* likes me, but it means a lot. I haven't taken it off since he gave it to me."

"I wish I'd gotten a Christmas present from a guy," Rhonda said wistfully.

"You did." Dawn scooted off the bed and returned to her closet. "This is from Keegan." She placed the neatly wrapped package on Rhonda's lap.

Rhonda smiled. "Aw . . . he shouldn't have."

She unwrapped a cute photo of Keegan and herself in a hand-painted frame, a snapshot Rob had taken in August and Katie had had enlarged. On the back was Keegan's baby handprint. "We're both so adorable," Rhonda said. "Maybe I'll wait for him to grow up. I'm positive I'll still be available."

Dawn giggled. "Yes, but will he be?"

Rhonda made a face, then said, "I wish we could go to the mall together tomorrow. Great after-Christmas sales, you know."

"Sorry, I'm not ready to venture out yet."

"Well, you can't hide in this house for the rest of your life. Sooner or later, you've got to venture out."

"Later," Dawn said, stroking the sweater. "Much later," she added under her breath.

Once Rhonda had gone, Dawn flipped on the television atop her desk and saw that the parade in Orlando was in full swing. She lay on her bed and watched for almost an hour before she heard the announcer say, "And here comes a band from Hardy High, in Columbus, Ohio. Don't they look sharp!"

Dawn watched Jake and his football buddies saunter across the screen. They wore their jerseys, and two of them held poles with a beautifully stitched banner proclaiming HARDY HIGH STINGRAYS. Jake waved to the camera, and Dawn's heart thudded as she imagined that he was waving at her as he had promised. Then her heart skipped a beat as she saw the cheerleaders coming behind him with the band following, playing a spirited march.

When the cheerleaders were directly in front of the camera, they stopped and went into one of their routines, a pyramid that featured Tasha at the top, poised like a bird about to take flight. The group shifted and Tasha made a spectacular dive into Jake's waiting arms. The onlookers clapped and whistled. Tasha struck a pose; then Jake flipped her and set her on the ground. Without stopping to catch her breath, Tasha did a tumbling run that ended with two somersaults and a back handspring. Again the crowd went wild.

"Wow!" the TV announcer said. "That little lady is quite a performer."

"I'll give her a ten!" the other announcer agreed.

Dawn stared at the screen without even seeing the band from her school strut past. Like a video-tape on an endless loop running through her mind, all she saw was Tasha's flawless performance. All she saw was Tasha's electric smile and perfect, limber body. Dawn stared down at her useless hand, felt a catch in her throat, picked up the remote, and turned off the television.

In February, Haley switched Dawn from a walker to a cane. At first Dawn felt stupid, like an old lady. Rob told her she looked cool, and by the end of the month Rob and Mr. Rochelle had created three canes in their woodworking shop, formerly known as the garage. Each was made of a different kind of wood, each had a head in a different shape that Dawn could easily grasp. One was a duck's head with a curved bill; the second was a smooth, flat handle; and the third sprouted a glass door-knob that easily fit the palm of her hand.

Snow and ice meant treacherous walking, and slipping became a constant fear that Dawn used as an excuse to remain indoors. Except for going to re-hab, she opted to not go anywhere, despite Rhonda's begging, "Can't we go to a movie together? Cripes! It's dark in a theater. No one can see you."

Dawn wouldn't budge. "I have movies sent to the house from the Internet," she said.

"Not the newest ones," Rhonda countered.

"I don't care. I don't want to go out in public. That's final."

Dawn didn't see much of Jake, which she decided was for the best. Between rehab and schoolwork, she didn't have time for wishful thinking. Except that she never really forgot about him. The bracelet on her wrist reminded her daily, but she didn't have the heart to take it off. At night, when she closed her eyes, she saw the TV screen from Christmas day. She saw Tasha in Jake's arms, and Tasha doing flips and hand-springs. She saw her own left hand, struggling to wad a piece of paper under Melissa's watchful gaze.

"Your nails look pretty," Melissa said during a work session one afternoon.

Rhonda had insisted on painting them a sparkly blue. "I can't do them myself," Dawn said to the therapist. "I wonder if I ever will again."

"But look how far you've come. You've graduated from yellow to red putty. The red is denser, harder to mush."

Dawn eyed the putty in her palm. "My hand always feels like I'm wearing a glove. And I still can't tie my sneakers."

"You're better," Melissa insisted. "And you'll improve more, believe me."

Dawn wanted to, but at the moment she felt discouraged. Her arm felt heavy, even though she exercised it diligently. And her fingers often refused to grasp, no matter how hard she tried to force them. Sometimes when she dressed she'd forget to put her left arm into a sleeve first and would have to start over again. Hard work was truly no guarantee that she'd recover totally from her stroke. And graduation was less than four months away.

* * *

By mid-March, Dawn had completed and passed the work for the grading period she'd missed while she was in the hospital. She had only to finish the current work to be caught up with her classes. Mrs. Gagliano sent home a note of congratulations, which pleased Dawn but also made her feel pressured to work harder.

One afternoon, after spending almost an hour on her home exercise bike, Dawn limped into the kitchen for a glass of water.

Her mother stood at the sink, scraping vegetables. "How'd it go today?"

"Slow. The same way it goes every day."

Dawn eased into a chair and drank her water.

"By the way, do you know a Brad Lewis?"

Dawn concentrated. The name was very familiar. "Why do you ask?"

"I heard on the radio this afternoon that a Brad Lewis, a graduate of Hardy High, had been badly hurt in a motorcycle accident. He rounded a corner and skidded on a patch of ice. I was just wondering if he might have been one of your friends."

Dawn closed her eyes, trying to bring up Brad's face. She couldn't, but the name . . . she *knew* that name. Suddenly her eyes flew open. "Oh my gosh."

"What is it?"

Dawn's blood ran cold. "That's Tasha Lewis's older brother."

Chapter
Fourteen

"Here he is." Rhonda pointed to the photograph of a smiling blond boy. They were in Dawn's bedroom, poring over the pages of Dawn's yearbook from their sophomore year, when Brad had been a senior. Almost a week had passed since Brad's accident. He was in a coma.

"He looks like his sister," Dawn said. She saw the resemblance in his smile and the shape of his jaw.

"Oh, he's far better-looking than his sister," Rhonda insisted. "I had a crush on him, you know."

Rhonda had had crushes on so many guys Dawn couldn't keep them straight, even before her stroke. "How's Tasha doing?" Dawn asked.

"She hasn't been at school all week, but her best friend, Susan Sawyer, said Tasha is a basket case. Tasha and her parents are practically living at the hospital."

"Look at his credits." Dawn referred to the long list of accolades beside Brad's name in the yearbook. "Soccer, gymnastics, honor student. A real achiever."

"He's on college scholarship for gymnastics," Rhonda said. "He was home on spring break. He was supposed to go to Florida, but he'd just been there with his family at Christmas, so he stayed home because it was his dad's birthday."

"How do you know all this?"

"It's all over school. Everyone's talking about it. And everybody's shook up about it too." Rhonda glanced sidelong at Dawn. "Um—Jake knew him pretty well."

"You mean because Jake is a friend of Tasha's, he's also a friend of Brad's."

"No. Jake really knows Brad. Anyway, I didn't think you cared about Tasha and Jake being together."

Dawn sniffed. "I don't."

"You should call Jake. He's upset."

"I don't know how I can help."

"He just might need a friend to talk to. He was there for you, wasn't he?"

Dawn felt a pang of guilt. At the very least, she

should call him. "I wouldn't know what to say to him."

"How about 'I'm sorry about Brad'? You'll think of something if you try."

"Maybe . . ." Dawn closed the yearbook, aware that her feelings toward Tasha were sensitive, like a sore spot that wouldn't get well. "You'll tell me what's going on, won't you? Keep me posted on everything you hear about Brad?"

"Sure," Rhonda said, giving Dawn a frosty glance. "Don't I always?"

Dawn did call Jake later that evening, after Rhonda had gone home. Her heart pounded as she held the receiver, and her mouth went dry when she heard his voice on the other end of the line. "It's me, Dawn," she told him.

"Hello." He sounded surprised.

"I—um—called because I heard about Brad Lewis, and Rhonda said the two of you were friends. I just want you to know I'm sorry. About his accident and all." The sound of her own breathing seemed to fill every inch of space in her room.

"I just came back from the hospital," Jake said. "Brad's up in the neuro ICU. His brain swelled, and he had emergency surgery last night. He's in a deep coma and on a respirator, too. The doctor has been really straight with Brad's parents—no sugarcoating about Brad's chances."

"What are his chances?"

"Slim."

She heard a tremor in Jake's voice, and her heart went out to him.

"His family's trying to decide whether or not to take him off the respirator."

"Oh," Dawn said, dismayed. Without a respirator to help him breathe, could Brad survive? "I'm really sorry."

"Tasha's hysterical. She and Brad were very close."

Dawn empathized immediately. What if it were Rob? She wouldn't have been able to stand it. "I didn't know you and Brad were friends."

"Remember when I moved back to Columbus when we were sophomores?"

Dawn would never forget his calling out to her that day as she was walking. Her heart had almost stopped. "I remember."

"Brad and I lifted weights together. He took me under his wing, helped me fit in with the jocks."

"Is . . . is there anything we can do?"

"No," Jake said. The finality in Jake's tone sent a shiver up her spine. "I'm going by the hospital before school in the morning to check on Tasha. She hasn't left his side for days."

Jake would have done the same for her, Dawn realized . . . if she had let him. That was the kind of person he was. Tasha needed him now. It would be selfish of Dawn not to want him to go and be with her. "Will you call me if anything changes?" she asked. "Rhonda will bring me updates, but you know how a thing gets bent around when too many people talk it over."

"You mean school gossip? It stinks! Rumors are flying around the place. I wish everyone would shut up about it."

"No one's doing it to be cruel. I think kids talk about it because it helps them deal with it." Dawn was surprised to hear herself defending the grapevine of gossip, which she'd loathed when she had been the topic of discussion.

"I know," Jake said. "Everyone's thinking, 'What if it were me?' It just doesn't make any sense, that's all."

"You mean the accident?"

"I mean *everything*. Why do things like this happen anyway? What did Brad ever do to deserve this?"

Dawn thought of Sandy, of Marlee, of all the kids she'd known with cancer who had died young. "It's a question I've asked a hundred times myself."

After a moment of silence, Jake said, "Trouble is, there's never any answer."

* * *

At rehab the next day, Dawn kept thinking about the hospital across the street, and of Brad lying in a coma up in the neuro ICU.

"You seem distracted," Haley said midway through Dawn's session.

Dawn told her about Brad.

"Yes, I've been up to see him."

"You have? But why?"

"In case he needs physical therapy."

"But I thought—I mean, the respirator and all . . ."

"According to tests, he still has brain stem function," Haley said. "His pupils react to light. He responds to pain stimuli. Frankly, we don't know what will happen when he comes off the respirator."

"You mean he might live?"

"It's a possibility. But even if he does, he's had extensive brain damage."

"Like me?"

"Not at all like you. You lost brain cells with your stroke, but he's lost all upper-brain function." Haley's mouth formed a grim line. "I just don't understand why a smart boy like that didn't take the time to put on his helmet. He wore a ski cap. Not much protection in a ski cap."

"Are you saying that if he'd worn a helmet, he would have been okay?"

103

"We have no way of knowing, but he sure would have had a better chance of being okay."

Dawn swallowed hard. "And you'll be his physical therapist? If he lives?"

"He'll need more help than I can give him, but yes, I'll be working with him." Haley pulled off her sweat shirt and dropped it on the floor. "Now let's get back to work, because I really can help you, which makes up for all the ones I can't help."

Dawn begged off her session early, and, like a moth drawn to a flame, she walked across the street to the main hospital. Katie wasn't due to pick her up for another thirty minutes, and Dawn was certain she could make it back to the rehab center in time. She rode the elevator up to the floor for neurology patients. One advantage of spending so much time in this hospital was that she knew her way around. She also knew how to act—pretend she belonged and that she had a purpose for being there.

No one on the neurology floor stopped her. No one even took notice of her. She assumed that her cane added to her credibility. Her heart thudded as she approached the intensive care unit, secured behind a door with a glass window. Dawn waited patiently, and soon a busy doctor buzzed himself in. Dawn followed in his footsteps. She walked slowly down the hall, the rubber foot on the bottom of her cane squeaking on the vinyl flooring. She glanced into the individual cubicles as she passed. Most were empty; others had patients with IV lines and wires hooking them to high-tech medical equipment.

At the end of the hall, she paused outside one large room where the most critical cases were placed. That was where she saw Brad Lewis, the only patient in the room, his bed directly in front of the nurses' station. Machines were positioned all around his bed. His head was wrapped in white bandages, and the respirator made a disquieting hiss. Two nurses worked on charts; another sat in front of a monitor.

Dawn knew she could go no further. Her heart was pounding crazily, and her palm was sweating so much that she could barely hold on to her cane. Her weak left leg felt rubbery; her right leg quivered with tension.

What was I thinking? She couldn't walk into this place and check out Brad for herself. It was crazy. What if a nurse saw her and questioned her? She'd been stupid!

She was about to retreat when, from behind her, a voice asked, "Who are you? And why are you staring at my brother?"

Chapter
Fifteen

Knowing that Tasha was standing behind her caused Dawn's blood to run cold. She felt cornered, and it was her own fault. Now Tasha would see her fully, would see the damage done to her body by her stroke. This was a nightmare coming true. Dawn took a deep breath and turned to face her adversary.

"Dawn Rochelle?" Tasha looked shocked, then confused. She also looked terrible. Her face was pale, her hair matted and limp. Her clothes were wrinkled, as if she'd slept in them. Large dark circles rimmed her eyes, which were red—undoubtedly from crying and lack of sleep.

"Yes," Dawn said, forgetting her embarrassment. How could she possibly be thinking about herself in front of this girl who was in such obvious pain?

"What are *you* doing here?"

"I—I hope you won't be mad at me. I was at therapy and I'd heard about Brad and I came over to see if there was anything I could do. Or if there was anything I could bring you." Her excuse sounded lame.

Fresh tears welled in Tasha's eyes. She wiped them with the back of her hand. "There's nothing anybody can do. Brad's never going to be well."

"I'm really sorry."

Tasha sniffed, then looked Dawn over head to toe. "I haven't seen you for months." Her gaze settled on Dawn's cane. "You doing better?"

"I'm doing better. Lots of hard work, though."

Tasha glanced over her shoulder at her brother. "We only get to visit him for ten minutes once an hour. Mom and Dad are in the waiting room." She gestured toward a closed door behind them. "It's my turn now."

Dawn stepped back self-consciously. "I shouldn't cut into your time."

Tasha nodded, gave Dawn a sad look. "I guess it's okay if you came. I haven't seen anybody from school except my best friend, Susan. And Jake. It reminds me that there's a normal world out there."

"I know the feeling."

Tasha drifted into the darkened room and to

the side of her brother's bed. Dawn watched through the window as Tasha bent over Brad, smoothed his forehead, and kissed his cheek. He never moved. Dawn dropped her gaze, feeling suddenly like a voyeur, watching things she shouldn't be seeing. She pulled herself upright, clutched her cane, and *tap-tap*ped her way back down the hall to the elevator as quickly as she could, the hissing of the respirator in her ears like harsh, cold rain.

"I felt about two inches tall." Dawn was telling Rhonda about her meeting with Tasha over a burger and fries the next day. "She hardly saw me, she was so broken up about her brother. She considers me a part of the normal world." Dawn laughed mirthlessly. "Imagine that? Me. Like this. Normal."

Rhonda's eyes were saucer-round as she listened. "Boy, that took guts. For you to go up there, I mean."

"No . . . it took a major dose of the stupids. I shouldn't have gone. I felt like an intruder. Like a thief stealing Tasha's time and energy."

"Don't be so hard on yourself. You were curious. Who isn't?"

"I know she'll tell Jake."

"Are you afraid he'll be mad at you?"

Dawn wasn't, but she did think he'd be baffled. She'd gone to such pains to shield herself from the rest of the world, and now she had barged into a sensitive, sorrowful situation where she didn't belong and had been seen by the one person she'd wanted most *not* to see her. "I don't think Jake has a clue that I've never been friends with Tasha. And now that I've thought about it, I'm not sure what I really have against her."

"Are you kidding? She's, like, totally a princess. And she's been hot and heavy after Jake all year."

"So that's why I should hate her? Because she likes the same guy I like? I'm telling you, Rhonda, if you could have seen her yesterday in that ICU with her brother, you'd have a whole different opinion of her. She didn't look like a princess yesterday."

"So what are you saying? That now you're going to be her best friend?"

"No, that slot's taken. Now and forever if you'll have me! There's no one on earth like you. But I can be nice to Tasha. She's going through a horrible time right now."

Rhonda gave a half-guilty shrug. "Don't let pity cloud your judgment. I doubt she'd have been nice to you if she'd run into you under different circumstances. By the next day in school she would have told everybody everything about you. And isn't that the reason you don't want to come back to school? You don't want everybody talking about you?"

That had been Dawn's biggest fear, all right, but at the moment it seemed petty. Why should she feel ashamed of something that had happened to her that was out of her control? What did it matter if someone said something mean about the way she walked or the way she looked? What kind of a person made fun of somebody because she had been maimed by illness or an accident, anyway? Would anyone be making fun of Brad Lewis? She doubted it. "I can't control what people say," Dawn told Rhonda. "All I know is that seeing Brad and knowing what his family's going through makes me glad that I can still walk and talk and think. And I also know how I'd feel if that accident had happened to Rob. Tasha's hurting. And it doesn't matter what she might have said about me. What matters is what I say about her. And right now, compared to her, I'm the luckiest person in the world."

Rhonda popped a French fry into her mouth and grinned. "Now you're sounding more like the Dawn Rochelle I once knew. And I have to say, I've missed her."

Dawn returned Rhonda's smile. "You know

what? I've missed her too. But starting right now, *she's back.*"

Dawn was struggling over a long reading assignment on Saturday afternoon when Jake called her. "Thanks for rescuing me from homework," she told him, her pulse racing at the sound of his voice. "How are you?"

"I've had better days."

"What's wrong?"

"I just got home from visiting the hospital." His voice sounded thick and his words were halting.

Fear shot up her spine. "You saw Brad?"

"His family opted to turn off his respirator."

"Oh." She shut her eyes, saw Brad lying immobile on the hospital bed in ICU. "Is he—I mean, did he . . . ?" She couldn't get the word out.

"Dead?" Jake asked. "No. He didn't die. He started breathing on his own."

"But that's a good thing, isn't it?"

"He's not conscious. In fact, his doctor says that according to all Brad's tests, he'll never be conscious again. Brad's in a 'persistent vegetative state'—that's what the doctor called it. You know what that means, Dawn?" Jake didn't wait for her to answer. "It means Brad will never wake up.

Never talk to his family or friends again. He'll never stand up, or look out a window, or see the sky, or smell the rain. He's got a tube sticking out of his stomach so they can feed him. He's a vegetable. A nonperson. He'll live out the rest of his life in a nursing home."

Tears instantly welled in Dawn's eyes. "Oh, no. Th-that's terrible."

"What kind of a life is that? Tell me, Dawn. What kind of a life is that?"

Chapter
Sixteen

In April, at the beginning of the final grading period, Dawn called and talked to Mrs. Gagliano. The principal told her that both her private tutor and her homebound teacher had recommended that she return to classes. Her tests, assignments, and papers were progressing well enough for her to remain on grade level. Dawn rode with Rhonda her first day back. Rhonda let her off directly in front of the main entrance, promising to park and hurry back with Dawn's books.

As Dawn got out of the car, she felt nervous, but she wasn't scared and she wasn't ashamed. She held her head high, ignoring the glances kids gave her and her cane, and made her way to the brick wall along the steps to stand out of the flow of foot traffic. The day was sunny and promising warmth. Dawn noticed the daffodils blooming in nearby flower beds. The air held the just-washed smell of spring.

She had already avoided one disaster the day before returning, when her dad had said, "Hey, I'll paint your cane with school colors! How about stripes in alternating bands?"

She'd blanched, shot her mother a panicked look. "Dad, that's a cool idea, but I really think I'd like to keep the cane the way it is."

"But why?"

Her mother stepped between them. "I think there may be a rule about only using school colors with the principal's approval."

"That's a dumb rule," her dad said.

"Well, you know kids . . . they can get carried away. It's for the best, honey." She patted his shoulder and gave Dawn a smile.

Dawn mouthed "Thanks."

Now, as Dawn waited for Rhonda, she kept her gaze trained on the flowers and willed her friend to hurry. But despite her best efforts to remain detached, a group of girls approached her. "Is that you, Dawn?" one asked.

"It's me." She recognized the girls from her classes. She eased the cane to one side and offered a smile.

"Wow, you look great."

"I do?"

"Hey, Heather!" one of the other girls called across the courtyard. "Come see who's back."

Within minutes, word had spread and Dawn found herself surrounded by classmates. Several of the girls—girls she hardly knew—hugged her, even shed a few tears. "We were so bummed out when we heard what happened to you," someone said.

"We're glad you're back," said another. "Neat cane."

"You'll be staying till the end of the year, won't you?" asked a third.

By the time Rhonda reached her, Dawn's head was spinning. She'd never imagined such a reception, never dreamed kids would have remembered her, much less missed her. Only the ringing of the first bell dispersed the group. When she and Rhonda made it inside the building, Mrs. Gagliano welcomed her warmly. "Take your time getting to classes," the principal said. "I've spoken to all your teachers, and you won't be marked tardy."

"How about me?" Rhonda asked.

"What about you?"

"Won't Dawn need someone to carry her books between classrooms? I'm volunteering."

Mrs. Gagliano considered the request.

"Um—it would be a help," Dawn said.

"All right. But," and she looked directly at Rhonda, "this isn't an excuse for you to dillydally and not make it to your own classes."

"Never entered my mind," Rhonda said.

When both girls were on their way to first period, Dawn said, "What was *that* about?"

"Helping. Don't you think you'll need some? How can you carry books and manage your cane when your left arm is still weak?"

Dawn slowly made a fist with her left hand. Rhonda was right. Her hand was still weak and often spastic. There was no way she could hold on to heavy textbooks and walk. "I thought I'd just stuff everything into my backpack."

"It would weigh a ton," Rhonda said. "You'd get real tired of lugging it, for sure."

Dawn cut her eyes in Rhonda's direction. "Maybe I should get some of the senior boys to make me a special pallet and carry me from class to class on their broad shoulders."

Rhonda giggled. "We could mount a crown over it, and when you passed everyone could bow and curtsy."

"That would work."

"And the guys can't wear shirts."

"Maybe some of them should. The wimpy ones."

"But not Jake and his friends."

They were laughing and late for class but not caring because it didn't matter. The halls had cleared, and by the time Dawn had gone to her locker, the final bell had rung. The reaction to her return had left her pleasantly surprised. No one stared and pointed, or whispered and made fun of her. Everyone seemed genuinely glad to see her. All the rest of the day, Dawn felt like a minor celebrity. After each of her classes, Rhonda was at Dawn's room scooping up her books while Dawn talked to kids who crowded around her. At lunch three boys offered to carry Dawn's tray, but Jake showed up and even Rhonda deferred to him.

"Glad to be back?" he asked.

"I am. I didn't expect such a welcome."

"I tried to tell you people cared."

"It was hard to believe when I felt helpless in the hospital," she admitted. "My mind was foggy, and the last thing I wanted was people feeling sorry for me."

"There's nothing wrong with someone feeling sorry for you. You feel sorry about Brad, don't you?"

She nodded. "That's true, but when you're the one people are feeling sorry for, well, you can't help wishing they would stop it. You want them to remember you the way you were, not the way you are."

"But people's brains are into the 'right now', not the 'used to be'. Which is good for me, or no one would have gotten over my missing that field goal. Now that soccer season's starting, everybody's looking for me to slap goals into the net. They aren't saying, 'He'll probably miss like he did the field goal.' "

She supposed what Jake was saying was true: People had short memories. Yet she also knew that an image could make an impact on the mind like a meteor slamming Earth from outer space. If the image was really graphic, really horrifying, it left an indelible impression. She doubted that she would ever forget the image of Brad hooked to machines and Tasha leaning over him. Even now, a month after being taken off the respirator, Brad remained in an extended-care nursing facility, alive but not alive, dead but not dead. She knew Jake went to visit him, but he didn't talk about it.

"Tasha," Jake said, his gaze focusing over Dawn's head.

He stood, and Dawn turned to see that Tasha had come up behind her. The hair on the back of Dawn's neck stood up because she'd been remembering the hospital scene so vividly. Had Tasha read her mind?

"Hello, Dawn," Tasha said.

If seeing Dawn with Jake bothered Tasha, it didn't show in her expression. She looked thin, almost haggard, and gone were the perky smile and the shine in her eyes. "Hello to you," Dawn said.

Tasha asked, "I was wondering if we could talk?"

"Um—sure. When? Right now, I've got class—"

"After last period," Tasha interrupted. "We both have gym, and I thought maybe you could hang around for a little while."

"Rhonda's driving, but I'm sure she won't mind waiting a little while extra." Rhonda had slipped away once Jake had settled beside Dawn in the cafeteria, but Dawn knew she'd see her friend after the next class and could clear it with her then.

"All right, then," Tasha said. "I'll wait for you in the locker room."

Dawn watched Tasha walk away, a cold, hard knot forming in her stomach. What could Tasha Lewis possibly have to talk to her about?

Chapter
Seventeen

Dawn was assigned a study hall instead of gym last period, but she made her way to the locker room as soon as the final bell rang, Rhonda dogging her heels.

"Want me to hide in the showers?" Rhonda asked. "I could listen and if it gets ugly, I could rush out and rescue you.".

"Rhonda, get a grip. Tasha just wants to talk, not murder me." Dawn slipped off her backpack and handed it to Rhonda.

"Are you sure?"

"I'm positive. Can you just wait out front for me? I'll come as soon as I can." The sadness on Tasha's face had haunted Dawn all afternoon. Dawn had seen enough anguish on the faces of her friends at cancer camp to recognize "soul torture" when she saw it.

"Jake's just outside on the soccer field. You can yell for him if you need—"

"Forget it. I'll be fine." Still, despite her assurances to Rhonda, Dawn felt edgy. She and Tasha traveled in completely different crowds, and, except for a few cool looks exchanged over Jake, they didn't know each other at all. Maybe Tasha was going to blast Dawn for appearing out of nowhere at the hospital to see Brad that day. If so, Dawn vowed she'd take it and keep her mouth shut.

By the time Dawn arrived, the locker room was clear of all except the smell of sweaty gym clothes and stale air mingling with the scents of soap, hair spray, and a spring bouquet of perfumes. Dawn found Tasha straddling a long wooden bench between two banks of lockers. Dawn said, "Hi. I got here as soon as I could."

"Thanks for coming."

Dawn eased onto the bench. Tasha's face was still damp from the showers. She wore no makeup, and her clothes looked as if they'd been pulled on hurriedly with no regard for neatness. Dawn licked her lips. "You doing all right?" she asked, breaking the awkward silence.

Tasha shrugged halfheartedly. "My brother's physical therapist is Haley Conroy. She said she knew you."

"I know her real well. I don't have to go to re-hab as much anymore, but I used to see Haley al-most every day."

"Is she good?"

"She's the best. Really, I'm not just saying that. She really cares about her work. And her pa-tients."

"She's showing us how to exercise Brad's arms and legs—me, Mom, and Dad. If he doesn't get stretched out, he'll get frozen joints and liga-ments."

Dawn felt a wave of pity. "It's necessary. I had to relearn standing and walking. It was hard at first."

"Brad moans when he's stretched. I think we're hurting him." Tasha pierced Dawn with a sharp look. "I don't want to hurt him. I don't want any-one hurting him."

Dawn toyed with her cane, running her hand across the smooth wood, trying to choose words that expressed honesty without ignoring Tasha's concern. "I'm not going to tell you it doesn't hurt. It does. Sometimes I cried because it hurt. And I felt really frustrated because I couldn't do things like I used to do. But I'm telling you the truth, if I hadn't stuck with the program, I would still be sit-ting in a wheelchair."

Tears shimmered in Tasha's eyes. "I keep

thinking he's going to wake up. He moans and moves, and even opens and shuts his eyes. But his doctor says he's never going to be . . . normal."

"Then that's all the more reason to keep up his therapy program. He needs it more than ever because he can't do it for himself."

Tasha nodded, turning her face away. "That's all I wanted," she said, dismissing Dawn with a wave of her hand.

Dawn saw that Tasha was struggling not to cry. She stood and picked up her cane. But she felt unsettled and wished she could say something reassuring. "The most important thing is letting the person know you love him. My family did that for me, and it made all the difference. The hurting part wasn't nearly so bad when I knew that everything everyone was doing for me was because they cared, because they wanted the best for me."

"Brad doesn't even know us." Tasha's voice caught.

Dawn squirmed. Had she made it worse? "Maybe he can't communicate, but he knows when someone touches him with love and caring. I knew it." Impulsively she added, "You see, I died once."

Tasha looked startled by Dawn's confession. "You *died?*"

"My heart stopped beating, and the hospital

had to bring in a crash cart to zap me. I might have stayed dead, but Rob, my brother, kept calling to me. I heard his voice like an echo in a canyon and I knew he wanted me to come back. I *had* to go to him. I don't know if I would have lived if he hadn't kept saying my name and forcing me to return to the world of the living. I came back because I loved him.

"I'm telling you this because possibly Brad can hear you. And I'll bet he can experience your feelings through your touches. Nothing can take the place of love. And that's the truth." Dawn turned and limped to the door. "If you ever want to talk, I'm available," she said.

Tasha didn't answer.

Dawn left the gym, her heart aching for the cheerleader whose whole world had crumbled the day a motorcycle crashed and a brother "died" to the world of conscious thought and everyday life.

Dawn asked about Brad Lewis the next time she saw Haley at rehab.

"Sometimes I take private-care patients," Haley said. "I agreed to work with Brad because his parents asked me to while he was still in the hospital and because he's going to need professional care for the rest of his life. I want to get him off to a good start."

"What is a vegetative state?" Dawn wanted to know. After her talk with Tasha, she had kept thinking about Brad's brain injury and how it differed from hers.

"Total lack of consciousness. Actually, the patient has normal waking and sleeping cycles, but those functions are controlled by the brain stem. So the patient breathes, has a heartbeat, has reflexes and can respond to pain, but he completely lacks upper-brain function—which means he can't think."

"So he's brain-dead?"

"No—that's different. A person who's brain-dead doesn't have the ability to breathe on his own, and once life-support machines are turned off, the person dies."

Dawn shuddered. "His sister told me that he moves, even opens his eyes."

"Such patients can be responsive," Haley said, scooping up a pile of red therapy putty and poking plastic pieces into it for Dawn to pluck out with her left hand. "A loud noise can cause them to startle, and sometimes they thrash their arms and legs, but it doesn't mean anything—the movements are random and without purpose."

"How do you know?"

"We have tests that measure responsiveness."

"Maybe the person's just trapped. Like being

locked in a room and not being able to find the door out."

"You're assuming they have the ability to form ideas. In a vegetative state, this simply isn't true."

"So where do you fit in?"

"A patient's body has to be cared for, and without proper exercise the muscles atrophy and tighten." Haley hunched over and curled her arms inward to demonstrate. "A therapist works to keep that from happening. If patients aren't turned on a regular basis, they develop bedsores. And their feeding tube has to be kept clean so it won't cause infection."

"I really feel sorry for Brad and his family."

"Me too," Haley said with a sigh. "This has got to be a parent's worst nightmare—to see their child beyond their reach, incapable of responding to them. I understand that he was a college gymnast and that he used to help his sister with her tumbling routines. Is she into gymnastics too?"

"She's a cheerleader," Dawn explained.

"Tasha's taking Brad's situation especially hard," Haley said. "When I go to the nursing center on weekends, she's always there. It isn't healthy. I was hoping she'd get back to a more normal life by now. Are you friends with her?"

"Um—more like acquaintances."

"If you have any influence with her, you might

want to encourage her to go on with her life and plans. Hanging around her brother's room isn't going to change things."

Dawn knew she wouldn't be able to say anything to Tasha. Tasha had dropped out of all extracurricular activities, even cheerleading. She showed up at school, went to classes, and left. Not even her best friend, Susan, could get her to join in senior activities.

"Now," Haley said, pointing to the mound of putty, "let's get on with your session. How about using that left hand to pick out those plastic pieces?"

Dawn was glad to stop thinking about Brad and Tasha and concentrate on a skill she was still fighting to master. She was grateful that, although damaged by the stroke, her mind was still under her control. She could think. She could reason and remember, react and respond. She was as different from Brad as day from night.

Chapter Eighteen

❦ ❧

"Do you want to go to the prom with me?" Jake asked. He was leaning over Dawn as she spun the dial on her locker. The halls had cleared, and he'd asked at lunch to drive her home after school.

Caught off guard, Dawn wondered if she had heard correctly. The prom. With Jake. "I—um—I can't dance," she said, then groaned over her inane comment. Of course she couldn't dance. Wasn't it obvious?

Jake grinned. "No problem. I can't dance either."

"Then we should go and not dance together," she said, feeling elated.

That night she told Rhonda on the phone. "Lucky you," Rhonda said with a sigh. "I heard today that Ed's asked Susan, so that dream's gone."

How Rhonda had ever hoped Ed would ask her confounded Dawn. The two of them never even talked unless Rhonda spoke first. "Anyone else you'd like to go with?"

"As if I'll get asked. I have the distinction of not having had a single date in my entire senior year." Rhonda sounded glum.

"Don't give up. Maybe some guy will wake up and see how special you are and ask you."

"Who? Rip Van Winkle?"

But three days later Rhonda called to say, "Ricky Manchester asked me to the prom today."

"That's great! You don't sound very excited."

"Ricky's kind of a nerd, but what choice have I got? If I want to go, he's it. Plus, we're going to double with one of his nerdy friends and then going to some all-night party with a bunch of parents chaperoning." She brightened. "But a date's a date. Just promise me you'll hang with me at the dance."

"I can't imagine hanging with anybody else," Dawn assured her, glad that Rhonda would be going and that she wouldn't be feeling sorry for her best friend because she had a date and Rhonda didn't.

That weekend Dawn and Rhonda went shopping for dresses far away from their neighborhood mall. "I won't look like everybody else," Rhonda insisted. Armed with a list of trendy boutiques, she had picked Dawn up early.

"What goes with a cane?" Dawn asked, poking through the racks at the first store.

"Better question—what's big enough to cover my butt?"

Dawn giggled. "You're too hard on yourself." She held up a long creamy-yellow dress. "Try this."

In the dressing room Rhonda squeezed into the gown. "I look like a piece of summer squash, skinny at the top, plump on the bottom. But that dress looks great on you."

Dawn studied herself in the floor-length aqua dress that came with a matching sweater scattered with sequins. She lifted her thick auburn hair, imagining it piled in curls with long wisps framing her face. She wondered if Jake would think she was pretty—even with a stiff, awkward left hand. "This is the dress for me," she told Rhonda.

"Are you kidding? We've just started looking. You can't choose the first thing you try on!"

"Sure I can. This covers my gimpy leg and hides my left arm. What more can I ask of a dress?"

Rhonda looked disappointed. "Well, I'm not finished." She grabbed a long pink dress off its hanger. As she climbed into the dress, she asked, "Did you hear that Tasha refused all invitations? Like she had about ten. She said she won't go. She's spending the evening with her brother."

Dawn hadn't heard but instantly wondered if, under different circumstances, Tasha might have been Jake's first choice. "She should go."

"Why? She's like a ghost around the school anyway. I've heard that she had a partial scholarship to some college in Texas for cheerleading." Rhonda rolled her eyes. "Who knew they even gave scholarships for cheerleading? Anyway, she said she's not going to take it."

"Not going to college?" Dawn felt a twinge of envy. Her own college plans had been sidetracked. Instead of applying to Ohio State as a premed major, she'd had to adjust her goals and settle on attending the local community college—at least until she was completely well and able to live on campus.

"That's what I've heard. I know what's happened to Brad is awful, but I think she's taking it way too hard." Rhonda checked her image in the mirror and moaned. "Terrific. Now I look like a wad of chewed and spit-out bubble gum."

"Stop trashing my best friend," Dawn said.

Rhonda went to find another dress, and Dawn thought about what both Rhonda and Haley had observed concerning Tasha. She wasn't adjusting to Brad's tragedy. Her grief was consuming her. Dawn understood that what had happened to Brad was horrible. But she couldn't help wondering why Tasha was putting her whole life on hold, when it couldn't possibly make any difference to her brother's well-being. Dawn had learned a valuable lesson when Sandy died. No amount of self-sacrifice could resurrect the dead. Life was for the living. It went on—with or without you, regardless of how much you tried to hide from it.

The look on Jake's face when he picked Dawn up on the night of the prom told her that she'd made the right choice with her dress. He slipped a corsage over her wrist; then the two of them tolerated Dawn's parents taking endless photographs. "You sure you're up to staying out all night?" her mother asked as Dawn and Jake edged toward the door.

"Haven't we hashed this out already? I've missed every other event this year. I don't want to miss this one." She and Jake were going to Susan's party at the country club after the dance, then to the traditional senior breakfast put on by the teachers in the school gym.

"Um—drive carefully," her father called as they got into Jake's car.

Jake backed the car out of the driveway. "You look terrific," he said above the beat of a salsa band CD.

"You too." His black tux made him look even more handsome to her than usual. She thought back to her long recovery in the hospital and rehab. At the time, she would never have believed she'd even be going to the prom, especially with Jake Macka. She prayed she'd make it through the evening without any relapses, because whenever she became tired, her speech slurred and her thoughts scattered. She didn't want to embarrass herself, or Jake.

The downtown hotel where the prom was being held was ablaze with lights. The lobby soared up three stories, with a winding staircase that led up to the mezzanine, where a huge ballroom had been decorated to resemble a scene from the 1950s. The dance committee—made up every year of the cheerleaders and the pep club—had gone all-out. Life-size cardboard cutouts of fifties rock-and-roll stars and movie stars had been placed next to tables. Five vintage cars were positioned around the perimeter of the room, showcased by spotlights and bright balloons.

"How'd they get cars up here?" Dawn asked, wondering how much input Tasha might have had into the planning of the dance.

"Freight elevators," Jake said. "Neat, aren't they?"

Photographers were taking memory photos for seniors beside the car of their choice. Dawn tucked her cane behind her skirt and stood with Jake by a gleaming chrome and aqua-painted '57 Chevy with pearly white leather seats. "Because it matches your dress," he said. "And your eyes."

A live band played fifties music, and colored lights flashed over the crowded dance floor. "I'm sorry about not dancing," Dawn told Jake as they watched.

But when a slow song played, he took her in his arms. "Lean on me," he said.

No problem, she thought. Held tightly by Jake, swaying to the music, she felt as if she were floating in a dream. His lips brushed her temple. Through the haze of total contentment, she heard a persistent beeping. Jake stopped, reached inside his tux jacket, and extracted a pager.

"You brought a beeper to the prom?" Dawn could hardly believe it.

He peered at the readout. A worried frown crossed his face. "We've got to go," he said.

"Where?"

"To the hospital. This is Tasha. Brad was admitted this afternoon with pneumonia, and I asked Tasha to page me if he took a turn for the worse."

Dawn went hot and cold all over. "B-but it's prom night."

"I know." Jake's expression turned apologetic. "I'm sorry . . . don't be angry. Will you come with me? Please."

"Yes," Dawn said, quickly making up her mind. As they left the ballroom, she was caught up in a maelstrom of emotion. Her dream date with Jake was crumbling because Tasha Lewis was intruding into Dawn's life. But under the circumstances, how could Dawn resent her?

Tasha ran toward Jake the minute the elevator opened on the neuro ICU floor. She looked disheveled and distraught. "You're here! Oh, thank God you're here."

Jake took Tasha by the arms and forced her to look into his eyes. "What's wrong?"

"Brad's heart stopped, but they got it going again. Mom and Dad are in with him now."

The color drained from Jake's face. "But he's still alive?"

Tasha nodded. "He's back on a respirator because it's easier for him to breathe." She looked past Jake at Dawn. "The prom . . . I—I forgot . . .

I didn't know what to do. I shouldn't have paged you."

"You did the right thing," Jake said.

"It's okay," Dawn added, reliving for an instant her own brush with death. "Nothing else matters."

Jake led Tasha into the waiting room, sat her down on a couch, and put his arm around her shoulders. Feeling unnecessary and out of place, Dawn eased into a chair across from the couch.

"If Brad had died . . ." Tasha buried her face in her hands.

"But he didn't," Jake said.

She looked up, tears streaking her cheeks. "It's my fault. It's all *my* fault and you know it. The accident . . . everything. *My fault.*"

Chapter Nineteen

"Stop saying that. It isn't," Jake said.

Tasha would not be consoled. Jake pulled Tasha closer, let her cry against his shoulder. In the quiet of the room, her sobs were heart-wrenching. After a while her crying slowed, quieted. Jake glanced toward a tissue box on the table next to Dawn. Catching his meaning, Dawn fished out several tissues and handed them to him. He gently pushed Tasha upright and put the tissues in her hands.

She blew her nose, wiped her eyes. "I—I'm s-sorry."

"Crying blows off steam," he said. "Don't worry about it."

She stared down at her hands. Dawn saw that her nails had been bitten to the quick. "I should probably go back to the room," Tasha said. "Just to check on things."

Jake helped her up. "Want me to walk with you?"

She eyed Dawn, shook her head. "But could you stay? For a little while?"

He agreed, and Tasha left. Dawn could almost hear the thumping of her heart in the lonely silence Tasha left behind her. Jake sat heavily on the edge of the couch, undid his bow tie, and opened the top button of his elaborate dress shirt.

"What was that all about?" Dawn asked. "How could Brad's accident be her fault?"

Jake raked his hand through his hair and slumped. "He wasn't wearing his helmet that day because Tasha had borrowed it. She won't let go of this idea that she's responsible for Brad's head injury, no matter what I tell her."

"Please, Jake . . . tell me exactly what happened."

"The day Brad took that motorcycle ride, Tasha had gone for a workout on her mountain bike. She couldn't find her helmet. She borrowed Brad's."

"And that's why he wasn't wearing his helmet in the accident." Dawn recalled how upset Haley had been over the information. Now she better understood Tasha's overwhelming sense of guilt.

"That's why, all right. Tasha's convinced that Brad would have walked away from his accident if he'd only had on his helmet."

"Who else knows how she feels?"

"I'm the only person she's told."

"Why only you?"

"Her secret was killing her. I'm Brad's friend. She confided in me."

"She should talk to a counselor. The guilt won't go away on its own."

"How do you know?"

"I just know."

Jake rested his elbows on his knees and stared down at the floor. "I don't know what to do. Or how to help her."

Dawn also felt inadequate. She didn't know how to help Jake *or* Tasha. In her grief, Tasha had laid a huge burden on Jake, and now he was as helpless as she was. It wasn't fair to either of them.

Tasha slipped back into the room. "Brad's breathing easier—" She stopped talking. Her gaze darted between Jake and Dawn, and she stepped backward as if she'd been slapped. "You told her, didn't you?" she flung at Jake. "You were supposed to keep it a secret. Now she knows and so will everybody else."

Dawn struggled to her feet. "Don't. It's not Jake's fault. And it's not your fault either."

Tasha glared at her. "What do you know about blame?"

"I know that when my friend Sandy died and when my friend Marlee died, I felt . . . cheated. I'd been robbed of their friendships. And worse, I felt guilty because I was alive and they weren't."

Tasha's face went white.

Dawn knew that her words had hit home. A lump of emotion clogged her throat. "I felt guilty because all of us went through cancer treatments. But I lived and they died. End of story. And just when I thought it was all over, I had a stroke. Payback?" she asked. "The thought has crossed my mind."

"But you didn't take their treatments away from them," Tasha countered. "Like I took Brad's helmet."

Dawn kept her gaze level, her voice calm. "Because Brad owned a helmet, he knew better than to ride without one. But he did anyway. It was his decision. Not yours."

Tasha couldn't have looked more shocked if Dawn had thrown cold water in her face. It was obvious that the notion had never crossed Tasha's mind. "But I . . . but if he . . ."

"He could have waited for you to return. You can't blame yourself for someone else's choices.

You can't play 'what might have been.' What happened is over. It was an accident. You will have to let it go. And find the courage to get on with your life. Brad would want you to."

Tasha sank onto the couch, stared vacantly into space.

Jake moved to Dawn's side. "Dawn's right," he said. "Brad took the risk and he lost."

"It isn't fair," Tasha said.

"I totally agree," Dawn said. "I know a lot about that. Sometimes life isn't fair."

Jake crouched in front of Tasha and took her hands in his. "I know Brad isn't out of the woods yet, but no matter what happens, you can't keep beating yourself up. Don't let Brad's accident claim two victims." He stood and touched her shoulder. "Right now, don't you think you should be with your family?"

Tasha wiped her eyes on the wad of tissue she held, looked up at Jake, and took his hand. "Thank you for coming," she whispered.

"What are friends for?" He squeezed her hand.

Dawn watched his fingers slip out of Tasha's grip. In Tasha's expression, she saw sadness war with resignation.

"Goodbye, Jake," Tasha whispered.

Dawn heard Tasha's tone of wistful longing and

felt very sorry for the girl. Then Jake slipped his arm around Dawn's waist, and together they walked out of the room.

In the car, Jake slumped in the driver's seat and closed his eyes. "Forgive me?" he asked.

"What for?"

"For ruining prom night for you."

"It was your prom night too."

"I wonder if anyone missed us."

Dawn knew she'd have lots of explaining to do to Rhonda, who'd expected to see her at the dance. "Who cares? Besides, the night's not over yet." She glanced at the glowing dashboard clock. "It's only two in the morning. We have hours to go."

He cocked his head and studied her. "The dance is over. Did you want to go to the party at Susan's?"

"I don't think either of us is in a party mood."

"You're right about that." He put the key into the ignition. "Do you want me to take you home?"

"And miss breakfast in the gym? Are you kidding?" She wanted to make him smile, to forget the trauma of the evening.

"How about breakfast at the pancake house?

There's an all-nighter on the south side. We can sit and drink juice and coffee—talk. I don't think we've talked nearly enough this year."

"Sounds good to me."

He reached to turn the ignition key, paused. "You said the right things to Tasha up there. I've tried a hundred times to tell her it wasn't her fault, but she wouldn't listen. Maybe you got through to her tonight."

"I've been there," Dawn said. "Sometimes it helps to hear from somebody who's had the same feelings." Dawn slipped her hand over his. "You know, Tasha likes you."

"I like her too," he said in an offhanded way.

"No—I mean she really likes you." Rhonda was right. Jake didn't have a clue about Tasha's feelings for him.

Jake reached over and cupped his hand over Dawn's cheek. "She's always just been Brad's kid sister to me."

"She's pretty, the prettiest girl in school. All that blond hair . . ."

He ran his thumb over her lips. "I've always been partial to redheads myself."

Her heart hammered in her chest, and she felt as if she might melt into the upholstery.

He held her face gently between his hands and

gazed deeply into her eyes. "I'm going to do something I've been wanting to do since the ninth grade," he said.

Ninth grade, she fleetingly thought. She was certainly one up on him. She'd had a crush on him since fifth grade—had wanted him to kiss her ever since she was thirteen. Dawn closed her eyes as his mouth found hers. His kiss was long, warm, deep, and achingly sweet—everything she'd ever imagined, all she'd ever hoped for in her dreams about him for almost half her life.

Chapter
Twenty

❧ ✍

"Say 'cheese'!" Rob said, aiming the camera.

"Parmesan!" Dawn and Rhonda shouted in unison.

They were standing in the lobby of the civic auditorium, where Hardy High was holding its graduation ceremony—the one place big enough to accommodate the parents, relatives, and friends of more than five hundred seniors.

"Very funny," Rob said.

Katie and both sets of parents burst out laughing. Dawn and Rhonda took bows in their navy blue robes.

The overhead lights flashed, signaling the start of the ceremony. "We've got to go line up," Dawn said. "Don't want to be left behind."

Rob took one final photo, put his arm around

his sister, and said, "We're all proud of you, Squirt."

She smiled, kissed his cheek, and headed to her prearranged place in the long line of seniors preparing to march down the aisle. The class had spent a Saturday afternoon rehearsing for the ceremony, but their antics and horsing around during the rehearsal had now turned into subdued anticipation. They were ready—no one more so than Dawn. The only thing she didn't like was the way Mrs. Gagliano had moved her toward the front of the line to stand with the valedictorian and the honor students. Dawn had worked hard for her grades, but she wasn't graduating with honors.

"Shouldn't I sit alphabetically like everyone else?" she'd asked the principal at the rehearsal.

"I want you on an outside aisle where you'll be more comfortable."

Dawn had agreed that it would indeed be easier for her to manage her cane if she wasn't sandwiched in the middle of a long row when it came time to march up onstage for her diploma, but she still didn't like being set apart.

"When are you going to get rid of that thing?" Rhonda asked as they lined up.

"By the end of the summer, I hope." Dawn had grown to dislike the cane and wanted to be free of

146

it. She practiced walking without it but still found it useful when she climbed stairs or when her leg grew tired. Or when she needed to walk down the long aisle of the auditorium and ascend the stage.

"I told her we'd celebrate big-time when she's free of it," Jake said. He'd come up behind them; he caught Dawn around the waist and nuzzled her neck.

She went warm all over. Ever since prom night, they'd been almost inseparable, a couple, an item, a happening. *Jake and Dawn. Together forever*, he'd written in her yearbook.

"Can I celebrate with you?" Rhonda asked.

"You got a guy?" Jake asked.

"I was hoping you'd supply the guy. You know more of them than I do." After the prom, Rhonda had elected not to date Ricky. With school ending and both of them going away to different colleges, it hardly seemed worth the effort. "Come on, Jake, can't you help a girl out?" Rhonda pleaded.

Jake laughed. "This will be a BYOF party— bring your own friend."

"You're so cruel." Rhonda sighed dramatically and hurried off to take her place in line.

The strains of "Pomp and Circumstance" began to play. "There's our cue," Dawn told Jake.

"I'll meet you out here when this is over." Afterward, they were going out to dinner with their families and then to a movie with just each other. He kissed her forehead and hurried off to his position.

To her left, Dawn saw Tasha. They weren't friends. They'd never be friends, because of Jake, but Dawn had heard that Tasha was seeing a counselor, and Dawn was glad of that. Brad had recovered from his bout with pneumonia and been returned to the nursing facility, his permanent home. Because he was young and strong, he was expected to live a long time. The word *live* was an odd one but that's what Brad would do. Jake visited Brad faithfully, and Dawn never asked jealously, "Was Tasha there?"

Dawn followed the girl in front of her through the auditorium doorway. Rows close to the stage had been reserved for the seniors. Parents and onlookers filled the rest of the seats. As Dawn walked, leaning on her cane, she realized that the place was packed. She prayed she wouldn't stumble, fall on her face. She had a bad case of nerves by the time she took her aisle seat.

When the class was seated, Mrs. Gagliano gave a short welcome speech, followed by the introduction of the valedictorian. After the valedictorian's speech, once the applause had died down, the principal returned to the podium. "And now the time has come for you all to be rewarded for your twelve years of hard work." Seniors' robes rustled in anticipation. "But before we begin, I want to first hand out one very special diploma to one very special young woman."

Dawn felt the skin on her neck prickle.

"This young woman overcame some enormous obstacles to be here today, obstacles that might have defeated a less determined person."

Mrs. Gagliano wouldn't. She couldn't—

"When this student was just thirteen, she was diagnosed with leukemia."

Dawn felt her face grow hot.

"When she was fourteen, she underwent a bone marrow transplant. When she was seventeen, just this year, she had a stroke."

Behind her, the audience had grown quiet. Beside her, she felt the gazes of her fellow students turning in her direction. Dawn closed her eyes. How could Mrs. Gagliano single her out this way?

"She spent long hours in rehabilitation retraining her body. But she also worked very hard disciplining and retraining her mind. Against great odds, she made up almost two grading periods in order to graduate with her class today. I, the faculty at Hardy, her friends, and her family couldn't be more proud of her. So I'm asking her to come up now for her diploma and for the recognition she deserves." Mrs. Gagliano stepped from behind the podium. "Dawn Rochelle, we commend you on your achievement."

Flustered, Dawn stood. Music began to play. She'd walked partway up the aisle when she realized that she'd forgotten her cane. She stopped, unsure of what to do. If she returned to her seat, people might think she was confused. If she continued up the aisle, she wasn't sure she could make it onto the stage.

Then suddenly Jake was beside her, offering her his arm. "Lean on me," he whispered.

Gratefully she linked her arm through his, and together they continued up the aisle, up the steps and onto the stage.

Jake walked her up to a beaming Mrs. Gagliano and stepped aside.

"We're proud of you, Dawn. Congratulations." Mrs. Gagliano held out the diploma.

The audience began to clap. Like a wave caressing the shoreline, the applause swelled, filled the auditorium.

Dawn half-turned, saw her classmates' sea of robes. The senior class began to stand, until all of them were on their feet. Some of Jake's friends shouted, "Way to go, Dawn!"

Then the audience stood, all of them,

clapping, cheering for her. All for her. As if she had radar, she singled out the row that held her family—her parents, Rob, Katie. And beside Katie, she saw Haley.

They waved.

She grinned.

She'd done it. She'd made it. There was no need to feel embarrassed about being recognized because of it. She also realized that to take the packet with her good hand would mean giving the principal a left-handed handshake. She considered all the hours she'd practiced picking small objects out of therapy putty. And she made up her mind. Dawn extended her left hand, wrapped her fingers around the packet, held on to it for dear life. She firmly shook the principal's hand, turned to face the crowd, and raised the packet high over her head in victory.

Applause crashed around her like thunder, and Dawn Rochelle knew that her long journey back was over and her future was straight ahead.